CW00547774

Sparkling Snow

Book Eight of the
Coming Back to Cornwall series

Katharine E. Smith

HEDDON PUBLISHING

www.heddonpublishing.com
www.facebook.com/heddonpublishing
@PublishHeddon

 Katharine E. Smith is a writer, editor and publisher.

An avid reader of contemporary writers such as Kate Atkinson, David Nicholls, Helen Dunmore and Anne Tyler, Katharine's aim is to write books she would enjoy reading – whether literary fiction or more light-hearted, contemporary fiction.

Sparkling Like Snow is her twelfth novel and a continuation of this popular Coming Back to Cornwall series, which was originally intended to be a trilogy. Connections is Katharine's latest series, with book one (*Elise*) published in 2021 and book two (*Maggie*) well underway.

Katharine runs Heddon Publishing from her home in Shropshire, which she shares with her husband and their two children.

You can join Katharine's mailing list, get a free short story, and a free e-book of
Writing the Town Read,
by visiting Katharine's website:
www.katharineesmith.com.

For all young people who have had to live
through the 'covid years'.

Especially for Laura and Edward.
It has been a hard time, but you have been
brilliant. I have always been proud of you, and I
always will be.

Also for Nina, (possibly) my youngest reader!
Even if you do call me Kathie.

I hope that life gets bigger and better and
brighter for you all xx

Sparkling Like Snow

1

The music from *The Snowman* filters through to the kitchen, bringing with it a faint longing for my childhood days. Christmases past. I don't think it could ever be possible to recreate that excitement. But this year is maybe more exciting, in a different way, because Ben is old enough to be more aware of the celebrations, and certainly the presents, and he has a crowd of over-eager adults hoping to help him get into the spirit of things. One such adult being my dad, who is currently watching the Christmas classic with Ben, and I'll put money on his eyes twinkling with tears at the end.

"You OK in there?" I call through.

"Oh yes," Dad calls back. "We're grand, aren't we, Ben?"

"Can I have a drink, Mummy?"

"What's the magic word, Ben?" I hear Dad prompt.

"Please can I have a drink, Mummy?"

"That's more like it."

The music pauses and the pair of them appear in the kitchen doorway.

"Would you like a drink as well, Dad?"

"Love one, Alice, if it's not too much bother. Here, let me put the kettle on. You look busy."

I am busy. I'm trying to make some mince pies, which Julie was meant to do, but Zinnia's poorly, and she's had to take her to the doctor.

"Alice, are you sure you're up to this?" she'd asked me, semi-joking. She's well aware of my limited talents in the kitchen.

1

"Yes, thank you, I will be quite fine," I had huffed. "I am sure I can make mince pies, they can't be that difficult."

And I was right, kind of. It's not too difficult – yet somehow, it's taking me ages. I decided to be ultra-organised, and get out everything I need in advance, weighing all the ingredients carefully and organising them in order on the worktop like I've seen on TV (though unfortunately there is nobody to clean up after me, like the TV chefs have). Only now there's not a lot of space to work in, and the bowl of flour is balanced precariously close to the edge of the countertop.

Really, as these are for some of our paying guests at Amethi, I should have been using the kitchen there, where there is more than enough space, but I wanted to spend the afternoon with Ben. Now Dad has called round, it's been a bit of a blessing. I mean, I love the idea of baking with Ben: him standing on a chair to reach the counter, an oversized apron wrapped twice around him. Probably a cute little smudge of flour on his nose, and a warm, soft-focus glow to the room (that's the image I have in my head, anyway). But today is not the day for all that. I need to concentrate. I must get these pies right, and ready for this evening.

We have an extended family party staying at Amethi, renting the five-bed cottage, and one of the two-beds as well. It's all been booked and paid for by a lovely couple, Mike and Sheila Potter, who have stayed with us once before, and have now brought their whole family down for an early Christmas, as their children will all be with their in-laws on Christmas Day this year.

"It's just fallen like that, somehow," Sheila told me, conspiratorially. "I think Heather's worried about Mike and me being on our own for Christmas, but we'll get out for a walk with the dogs, and have a nice dinner, then a drink down the local – it's only two doors away, so probably more than one if I'm honest!"

"That does sound quite appealing," I'd mused, watching as our dog Meg rushed through the remnants of the wildflower meadows with Mike and Sheila's two spaniels, taking it in turns to chase and be chased.

Tonight, the plan is for the family to get together in the Mowhay, for a big meal, so I just hope that Zinnia is OK and that Julie isn't too long at the doctors. I may just about be able to cope with mince pies but I don't think I could stretch to covering anything else Julie has planned. With Jonathan living it up in Spain with Sam's sister Janie, we don't have many options if Julie ever does have to miss a day or two, but so far it has never come to that. We really ought to have some better contingency plans in place, though. Something else to add to the never-ending list.

Luckily, Mike and Sheila are so nice, and so pleased to have all their family together, that I think they will be happy with the pies however they turn out (unless they're burned to a crisp), but that actually makes me even more keen to get them right.

"Are you sure I can't help?" Dad asks.

"No, it's fine, thank you." I smile at him as he fills the kettle. "To be honest, it's as much about food hygiene as anything. I should really be doing these at Amethi, but sometimes needs must. Anyway, you're helping by looking after this little man," I swing Ben into the air, narrowly missing the bowl of flour. "Oops. Maybe I'll bring your drinks through to you, if that's OK."

"That's more than OK. Or I could take Ben to the Sail Loft, if you like? I know your mum would be thrilled to see him."

"Oh no, that's OK…" I think again. "Actually, Dad, that would be great. If you're sure you don't mind."

"Course not. And why don't we play it by ear? Let me know how Zinnia is, and if Julie's got back to work OK. Ben can stay for tea if he'd like to."

"You are a star, Dad," I say. "Thank you so much."

"Yes, well, you need to be taking it easy, really," he says, eyeing my rounded tummy. "But I know you don't like me telling you things like that."

He's right, on both counts.

I think again about making the pies here. Maybe I'll cut my losses and head up to Amethi now. It will be far easier, and just feels like the right thing to do. I pack up a few things for Ben and bundle him into his coat. Mum and Dad already have a car seat installed in their car, so I fasten him in, and kiss his nose, leaving the cute little smudge of flour there that I'd imagined. In the new year, I think, when I'm on maternity leave, while the baby sleeps I will do more things like baking with Ben. There'll be time for all that, I console myself, pushing the working-mum-guilt away and waving Ben and Dad off, then turning work mode on full.

❄ ❄ ❄

Meg leaps out of the car at Amethi, her nose high as she sniffs the air approvingly. She loves it here, with the fields and the woods, and so much space for her to explore. I know she won't go far, and I'm happy to let her trot off while I get out the box of ingredients from earlier – no point wasting them – and head off to the kitchen. It's dark and echoey, with no Julie, but I switch on the lights and the ovens, and the radio, and it's soon warm and cosy and companionable.

I message Julie:

Any news? xx

We're next in, I think. I hope. Z now full of beans.

Typical. Hopefully see you soon.

Yes, Luke's on his way home anyway so he can take over. I'll be with you shortly xx

☺

Right, I think, relieved that my friend shouldn't be too much longer, and I can go back home. I'm starting to feel tired. I rub my belly lightly, feeling an answering kick, and wonder if it would be cheeky to ask Mum and Dad to have Ben overnight. Sam and I could have a takeaway, and get a good night's sleep, and…

Enough! I tell myself.

First, the mince pies. They aren't going to make themselves.

2

There really is so much to do before Christmas. It all feels a bit stressful, if I let it. In the next few weeks at Amethi, we have the winter solstice yoga retreat (I don't think I will be doing much yoga this time round), Christmas, and New Year. All three major events in our business year, and all running on from each other. It's a great time, usually, and I love the thrill of the challenge, to get each very important and very different week just right. This year, that feeling is still there, but slightly muted because I'm so tired.

The solstice is on a Wednesday, with the Return of the Light celebration on Thursday morning, and guests clearing out later that day. The parties who are arriving for Christmas are getting here on the Saturday – Christmas Eve – so we have time on the Friday to make the houses Christmassy, adding trees, twinkly lights, and a few gifts for our guests. They will be here all week: the Coopers - a large family coming down from Shropshire, having the same two properties that Sheila and Mike have at the moment - then two individual couples. The Barretts are young and expecting their first child, and the Browns, a couple about my mum and dad's age, who, like Sheila and Mike, will be spending Christmas without their family this year.

While we don't normally cater much for Christmas week, the Coopers have asked if there is any chance that we could, and I think Julie actually is relishing the idea of providing a huge Christmas dinner. "It'll be a great challenge for me," she said, "and you don't have to be here for it. In fact, you mustn't. You have to be at home, with your feet up, being waited on by Sam. And that's that."

"We'll be at the Sail Loft."

"Of course! Well, even better. You'll have plenty of people to wait on you, and Ben will have Sophie to play with him."

"And will Luke and your mum be OK, without you?"

"They'll be fine! And they've promised to come and help clear up."

"Well, that's commitment."

"I know! It will be so nice to have Mum down. I can't wait."

"I bet she can't, either."

"She does seem pretty excited!"

"And what's Jim doing?"

"He'll be at the soup kitchen again." Luke's dad began doing this the Christmas after Luke's mum, May, died, and he's carried on, year after year. He says Christmas will never be the same again, so he might as well embrace the difference. "Then he'll come to us in the evening, but Marie's up at her boyfriend's parents' this year. Mum and Jim will spoil Zinnie rotten."

"Ha! I'm sure."

Meanwhile, Mum and Dad have decided to keep the Sail Loft shut for Christmas, and as far back as September had sent a formal invitation to me and Sam, to spend Christmas Eve and Christmas Day with them.

Dear Mr and Mrs Branvall,
Mr and Mrs P Griffiths of the Sail Loft Hotel request the pleasure of your company from Saturday 24th December – Monday 26th December, inclusive, as their esteemed guests.

You will be very welcome, and all meals will be provided.

Please bring your delightful son, and crazy canine, and a selection of gifts, particularly for Mr Griffiths.

They sent a similar invitation to Sophie, and she was delighted. "Have you got one?" she asked Sam.

"No, they're only inviting you."

"They're…?" This had knocked her slightly. I could see her imagining a Christmas spent with just my mum and dad. Then it clicked. "Oh, very funny, Dad."

"I know."

"So we're all staying at the Sail Loft?"

"Looks like it."

"That's so cool! Is Amber going to wait on us?"

Sophie's best friend is a weekend waitress at the Sail Loft, which sometimes seems so hard to believe. When Julie and I first came down to Cornwall, I was a waitress there. I was just a year older than the girls are now.

When we came back ten years later, Sophie was nine years old. We met Amber when she and her parents moved nearby, when the girls were eleven. Sometimes, I can't believe Amber has now got my old job. If I'm not very careful, I'm going to start feeling old.

"I think Amber will be at home with her family," I smiled. "And I'm not sure how she'd feel about waiting on you! I imagine you'd be one of those awkward customers who complain about everything."

"Oh yeah, definitely, if she was the waitress. And Phil's cooking, too. Can't make it too easy for either of them."

Mum and Dad have also invited Karen and Ron, for Christmas dinner, though I'm not sure how keen Dad is on this idea. "Can we tell them what time they have to leave as well?"

"Oh don't be a curmudgeon, Phil!" Mum chided him. "I'm sure they won't outstay their welcome."

I know Dad is thinking of the first Christmas we had with Karen back in Cornwall – she had outstayed her welcome then, and having had a 'drink or two', did not seem aware of that fact.

"Yes, Dad, don't be a *curmudgeon*!" I'd laughed. "Anyway, now Ron's around, Karen's very different. Much better behaved. And he seems to have a greater awareness of other people than she does. And if the worst comes to the worst, I'll kick them out, OK?"

"*Curmudgeon*," Dad had muttered. "Seems a bit unfair."

I can sympathise with Dad, really. Karen can be a bit… overbearing, shall we say? But she's really mellowed since she's been back, and it's not just down to Ron's influence. Also, Ben loves her. She has started having him with her one day a week, and he always comes back tired but happy – and it seems to have the same effect on her. I can't begrudge spending time on Christmas Day with her, and I know we'll all have fun.

The thought of being a hotel guest and looked after for a couple of days is endlessly appealing. There is much to do in terms of work but when Sam and I check in to the Sail Loft on Christmas Eve, it marks the start of a period of change when, all being well, we will become a family of five (including Sophie), or six (including Meg). Ben will be promoted to big brother, and I will finally meet this new little person who's taking up an increasing amount of space inside my belly. I just cannot wait.

When I pull the trays of mince pies from the oven, I feel unjustifiably proud. It is, after all, just three trays of mince pies. But they look good. Plump and golden – *deep and crisp and even*, I think with a small smile - and no signs of overcooking anywhere! I did follow Julie's very careful instructions, to the letter, and I wonder now if that's where I've been going wrong all these years. Thinking I can better established chefs and amend their tried-and-tested recipes with little twists of my own. I know, really, that I shouldn't do it, but I can't seem to help myself, somehow.

The kitchen is a bit of a mess, though. I'll need to tidy up before Julie gets here. She is very proud of her kitchen and quite fastidious about keeping it tidy, organised, and clean. Spotless, really. Which is important in a chef, but not something I'm very good at. Her latest text suggests I have about half an hour, and I think I deserve a little break, so I boil some water and fill a mug, adding a slice of orange (it seems more festive than lemon, somehow), and take it outside, to the seats in front of the Mowhay.

We will cover these up after New Year, when we close for a month, and we might expect winter to really get a hold on us, but right now it feels hard to imagine that it could ever get properly cold. Though the sky is entirely obscured by low-hanging cloud, the temperature is still in the mid- to high-teens, and it feels like early autumn. I fear that Ben may never get his wish of a white Christmas, unless we bite the bullet and take him to Lapland or somewhere one year.

I sit gratefully on one of the benches, watching the wisps of steam escape my mug. A colony of gulls drifts overhead – spaced out from each other, and utterly silent. They are ethereal and peaceful, in stark contrast to their noisy harbour selves, who squawk loudly from rooftops, walls and chimneys, and stalk and hunt for ice creams, pasties, chips… straight from unsuspecting tourists' hands.

I love to watch them like this (I secretly admire their cheeky seaside personas too, though I realise that's controversial). As they glide overhead, their V-shaped wings barely moving, I can see how they might pass as ghosts. Folklore has them as the souls of dead sailors, or fishermen, and there is a long-standing and deep-rooted belief that they should therefore never be harmed, much less killed. Even if they nick your bag of chips.

Sometimes, on a misty day, if I'm walking on the beach, or the high roads up at the top of the town, I imagine long-past days, the fishing fleet heading off to sea, seeming to shrink in size the further from shore they go; miniature in comparison to the vast waters. The weather might turn, as it can round here – *turning on a sixpence*, my grandma used to say – and the tiny vessels be swallowed up, the sea tossing a handful at a time into its greedy mouth. *Gulp.* They'd be gone.

I often think, too, of the ruthless wreckers, luring ships into shore with their false beacon lights. Letting them crash, leaving the crews to perish in the icy fathoms. It's no wonder that there are so many stories associated with this land, and the sea that surrounds it. The tin mines, the echoey caves, the vast moors and standing stones. It's a magical place, and bright with life in the sunshine, but just a little bit eerie on colder, mist-wreathed days and nights.

There is movement in the field close by, and it makes me start (must be all these thoughts of ghosts), but it's only Meg. She spies me, and trots through the knee-length stubble, gaining speed as she approaches.

"Hello, girl," I say, as she nuzzles me and plonks herself unceremoniously at my feet. I sit with her leaning against

11

my legs as I blow gently on my mug of water, watching the gulls until they are out of sight.

It's a gentle, grey day, and so still. So quiet. The cloud cover envelops the earth and the air softly, protectively. I know that in a moment I must heave myself to my feet and clean the kitchen, but I think, as I often do, of Lizzie urging me to be in the moment, and I resolve to do just that.

3

Just as I'm about to get up and return to the kitchen, I hear the sound of a car approaching. I get to my feet, fighting the urge to groan as I do so. Meg, ever-ready, leaps up nimbly, and follows me as I walk around to the gravelled car park. There are no other cars but mine there at the moment. The guests must all be out enjoying the mild weather.

I love Cornwall in the summer, but it has another quality in the winter, and I often think those people who come to stay out of season are in on a little secret. I just love the quiet, I suppose, and being able to walk through town unimpeded by throngs of people who stop with no notice to gaze into the Seasalt window, or pasty shop, or fudge parlour. If you check in on one of the local Facebook pages, you might be forgiven for thinking that all locals hate tourists (or 'emmets' as they are sometimes known, and not always affectionately), but it's just not true.

The population of the town ebbs and flows like the sea, so that at high season, in July and August, the resident population of around 12,000 is swamped by tens of thousands of people. This can cause problems, and some resentment, but by and large the majority of these people are very welcome. Not necessarily the ones who drive the wrong way along the narrow network of one-way streets, of course. Or those who block up said streets for an inordinate length of time while they unpack into their luxury accommodation. But I am so lucky to live here, and I never stop reminding myself of that fact. It would be a mean-spirited person who would truly begrudge somebody else the chance to enjoy a week or two in such a beautiful place.

"Hi!" I call to Julie, as she emerges from her car – a sleek black machine that is more than a few cuts above the rusty old red number we used to bump around in. Sadly, we had to say goodbye to that when it started to spew out plumes of black smoke from its exhaust.

"Hello!" she says, bending forward to scratch Meg behind the ears. "All OK here?"

"Yes, thanks. How's Zinnie?"

"She's alright. It's another ear infection."

"Poor girl."

"I know. But she'll be on the mend soon, hopefully."

"And Luke's back?"

"No, I just left her at home to fend for herself," she says sarcastically, and I pull a face. "How are those pies?"

"Oh my god, the pies!" I say, with a look of horror.

I watch my friend's expression change to one which is trying to conceal genuine concern. "They're fine." I put her out of her misery. "Just cooling in the kitchen."

"You bugger," she says, laughing as she approaches me. She links her arm through mine. "Come on then, I want to inspect them."

"As long as you don't inspect the kitchen," I say. "I was just about to clear up."

"Of course you were," she soothes, grinning.

"I was!"

"I believe you. Thousands wouldn't."

Meg goes her own way, sniffing around the gravelled courtyard area while Julie and I head to the kitchen.

"It was boiling in the doctors!" she exclaims. "I'm sweating."

"It's lovely, really," I say, "though it doesn't feel right for December, does it?"

"No. They say we're in for a hard January, though. Oh my god. I sound like an old woman. In fact, listen to us both, discussing the weather. We're definitely growing up."

"I don't know about that," I say. "But I quite like the thought of a cold January. We'll be off work. You and Luke will be away in India anyway, and Sam and Ben and I can settle down with this little one." I pat my tummy. "As long as I can get to the hospital and back, and we're all safe at home, I really don't mind if we get snowed in."

"Sounds quite appealing, doesn't it?"

"It does." I can picture the scene now. I feel so tired by this pregnancy, and looking after a toddler, and working. The thought of some time at home, where we are forced to do literally nothing but stay in and cosy and warm, seems like heaven. Of course, the reality would probably be that we'd drive each other mad after a day or two. Sam would be itching to work, or get out for a run, or on his bike. Ben would have played with all his toys by lunchtime on the first day and be bouncing off the walls, needing some outdoor play, and friends to enjoy it with. Still, I can dream, can't I?

I open the kitchen door, and swing my arm wide, gesturing to the racks of pies I have left cooling, and hoping to distract Julie from the flour, sugar, and splodges of mincemeat all over the stainless steel surface where I've been working.

"Well done," Julie is surprised, I can tell. "They look perfect!"

"Like me," I say. "Maybe I am growing up, after all."

"Oh no, I've already changed my mind about that. Just look at the mess you've left," she scolds, like she's my mum.

"Sorry," I say, mock-shamefaced. "I just got a bit distracted outside, that's all."

"Some passing clouds you just had to watch?"

"Seagulls, actually."

"There's no such thing as seagulls, Alice," Julie trots out one of Sam's lines. *"Just gulls. And these ones happen to live by the sea."*

While Julie starts to wipe the countertop, I move the trays of pies out of her way. But somehow I let one slip, and four of the pies fall out and faceplant the floor. "Shit!" I kick myself for not being more careful. Bloody fluffy pregnancy brain. It's been annoying me a lot lately, I've been thinking I've lost my keys when they've been tucked into the back pocket of my maternity trousers – and forgetting to book tickets for Ben's nursery Christmas play (honestly, tickets seem a bit over the top to me but that's not the point... I should have been more organised. Luckily, Julie was, and got some for me and Sam, though I don't think he's going to be able to come).

"They're ruined!" I sob.

"Alice, are you crying?"

"No."

"You are!"

"I am. But it's just hormones. Just ignore me. Let's get this cleared up. I'm so sorry, though. What an idiot."

"Oh, don't give it a second thought. There's still plenty of them. You need a rest, my friend. You shouldn't be working when you're so..."

"Stupid?" I suggest.

"No, not stupid... well, maybe a bit." She puts her arm around my shoulder. "Seriously, Alice, you should rest up.

16

I know that's easier said than done."

"It is. It's OK, though. I just need to get through the next few weeks, then I'm home and dry."

I lie awake some nights, getting ahead of myself. Wondering how Julie and I are going to manage Amethi after the baby has come. But I am tripping over my thoughts, looking well into next year, when in between now and then there is the small matter of giving birth, and looking after a newborn, and making sure Ben's OK with being a big brother. I have to stop, and take a breath, or three, or four, letting them out slowly and carefully while I get the thoughts straight in my head. I know that we can find a way to manage Amethi between us. Julie says she can take on more of my work, as Luke will be at home a lot more, and Zinnia's going to be in nursery an extra day a week anyway. It will be OK. We'll make sure it is. We will have to.

"OK," Julie says now, her eyes on mine, checking I really am alright. "But none of this is as important as your health, and your baby's."

"It is quite important," I sniff.

"Well, yes it is. Quite important. Very important," she concedes. "But you're still more important. And so is your baby."

"Thank you. Can I blow my nose on your jumper?"

"No, you can go and sort yourself out in the toilet, and then you can go home. I've got everything covered here."

"But I was going to see Sheila…"

"I can do it!" Julie insists. "Now go on. Shoo!"

"Thank you, Julie. You're the best."

"I am." She smiles and kisses me, then gently but firmly guides me out of the room. "I'll see you tomorrow."

I head into the toilet at the other side of the Mowhay,

17

and look in the mirror. My eyes are red-rimmed, and my face looks pale. I imagine getting home, getting changed, and just settling down on the settee. Maybe I will ask Mum and Dad if Ben can stay with them tonight. I have to push back guilt at the thought. I feel that I should be spending as much time with him as I can before his little brother or sister arrives.

If I just rest tonight, I tell myself, I will be recharged to have lots of fun with him at the weekend. Maybe we can go for a walk somewhere, with Sam. The thought makes me feel better, then a little bit tearful again.

I wash my face and look my reflection in the eyes. "Pull yourself together, Griffiths," I say, correcting myself: "Branvall."

Head high, I walk outside and whistle for Meg, who comes running. She leaps into the car, and I message my mum, asking if it's OK for Ben to stay with them tonight. Before I've even put the car in gear, the reply comes back:

Of course. I'm glad you've asked. Have a break. Dad said you were looking a bit tired xx

I feel like crying again, which is a sure sign I am over-tired. Relief washes over me as I head along the bumpy drive, knowing that back at home some quiet time and a pair of cosy pyjamas awaits me.

4

I love the run-up to Christmas. Possibly even more than Christmas itself, which is only two weeks away now! And it feels like it, in so many ways. The town is strung with thousands of lights. Each shop has a twinkling Christmas tree above its doorway, thanks to the Christmas Lights Committee, of which Dad is now a proud member. The star is on the top of the church tower, glowing nobly through the night, and until the sun is fully risen each morning. With the solstice fast approaching, we are at the time of year when daylight is scarce and all the more precious. By the time Ben comes home on his nursery days, there is just a small scraping of light left before the town falls away into darkness for another night.

Today is changeover day, although only two of the places are let this week. And then next week is the winter solstice yoga retreat. It feels like barely any time since the last one, but so much has happened this past year.

I look at Sam, lying comfortably asleep beside me. My mind fills with the familiar 'what ifs', as I think back to his accident in the summer. It is generally agreed that he was lucky to survive the fall down the cliffs onto the rocks – and very lucky to have survived it as well as he did.

As always, I tell myself that to wonder 'what if' is meaningless, and could be applied to every other situation, good and bad.

"I've seen folk perish from less than that," Ron, Karen's partner, and an RNLI stalwart, said to me on the quiet. To be honest, I hadn't needed to hear that, but I think he was quietly impressed by Sam's strength, health and resilience.

"It's his second near-miss," I told him, relaying what I knew about Sam's accident when he was a teenager, although that had happened after I had returned back up to the Midlands, and I'd only found out about it ten years later.

"Must have nine lives, that boy," Ron said.

"Well, let's hope we don't have to find out, eh?"

Now, Sam is well recovered, but has some residual back pain, which bothers him after a long day, and sometimes during the night, so that I am aware of him tossing and turning, even though I know he's trying not to disturb me. Between him and this baby, which really is a wriggly little thing, I am not getting a lot of sleep at the moment.

I would love to stay in our cosy bed, sharing the warmth of the duvet with Sam, and drift back to sleep, but that is not my fate today. Instead, I ease myself out from under the covers, and tiptoe to the little en suite bathroom.

I can hear Ben stirring in his room, and if I'm not quick, he'll be bursting through our bedroom door and waking his dad. Sam won't mind, but I want him to sleep. I want him back to full health, and as soon as possible.

I stealthily tiptoe barefoot across the soft carpet, and I'm just in time. As I open the bedroom door, I nearly walk right into Ben. He opens his mouth, but I scoop him up and shush him: "Daddy's asleep," I whisper into his ear, just managing to pull our door to behind me.

"OK!" he says loudly, though I suspect he thinks he is being the model of subtlety.

I smile, kiss his nose, and hug him to me, feeling his bed-warmed body against mine, and his little legs attempt to wrap around my waist. They won't go far at the moment.

"Shall we go and get some breakfast? Then do you want to come to Mummy's work?" I ask and he nods enthusiastically. "I'm going to have to put you down, though, OK?" He nods again.

I put him down, being careful not to overstretch my back. Downstairs, I can hear a familiar thud of tail against floor.

"Meggy!" Ben shouts, delightedly. Ah well, it's down to Sam now, whether he can sleep on through the sounds of the waking house.

Meg is stretching downstairs, ready to greet us. She licks Ben on the face, and he giggles then snatches his tiger toy away. "No, Meg, this is mine."

She seems to sense she shouldn't jump at me at the moment, and I could swear she has become more gentle, and protective of me, since I've been pregnant. They say dolphins can sense a baby's heartbeat in a pregnant woman and I wouldn't be surprised if dogs can do the same.

"Hello girl," I ruffle her head. "Shall I let you out?"

Ben climbs onto a chair at the kitchen table, while I open the door for Meg. I would love an icy blast of winter-cold air, but the temperature has remained stubbornly neutral for weeks now. There are still plants in flower in the garden, and it feels wrong.

Meg goes outside while I pour a glass of milk for Ben and put the kettle on.

"Porridge?" I suggest.

"Yes please, Mummy, with honey."

"Of course with honey!" I smile at him. "And banana?"

He shakes his head. "Just honey."

"OK," I sigh. He's gone right off fruit lately, but women older and wiser than me have said not to worry about it. It's hard not to, when the 'five a day' mantra runs on repeat through my head. No point letting it stress me out, though. I have quite enough to think about right now.

After breakfast, I plonk Ben and Tiger in front of the TV for a bit, while I have a shower. In the cosy semi-darkness of our bedroom, Sam sleeps on, so I use the family bathroom, and get dressed in Sophie's room, then grab some clothes for Ben, and head downstairs. He is watching a Christmas episode of one of his favourite programmes, *Ben and Holly*. He particularly likes the fact that one of the main characters is called Ben. Of course, it being a Christmas special, everywhere is covered in a thick blanket of snow. I don't think I've ever seen an actual white Christmas, and I don't know why this myth persists, but still, it's a nice idea.

"Is it a good one, Benny?" I ask, pulling him gently to his feet.

"Yes, yes, Father Christmas," he says, pointing to the screen.

"Oh yes!" I say, helping Ben pull his pyjama top off. There is a large splodge of porridge on the chest, so these will have to go in the wash. "He'll be coming to see us soon."

"Yes, and it's going to snow at Christmas."

"Well, I don't know about that, Ben. It doesn't really snow in Cornwall very often."

His face crumples a little.

"But you never know!" I add brightly. Why crush his dreams? By the time Christmas is here, the weather will be the last thing on his mind.

At Amethi, Ben exclaims at the sight of the outdoor Christmas tree. It's not as big as the ones we've had before, but we decided that getting a different tree each year is not really in keeping with our eco-friendly plans, and Lizzie helped us source a tree which we've had transplanted into the grounds, close to where we used to site the chopped-down ones. It seems to have settled well, and is now decked out in lights and baubles, and looking very grand.

Meg, slightly less impressed, wees on the ground underneath its branches.

The previous week's guests are industriously trotting to and from their cars, with bags and boxes.

"How is it possible that we are leaving with more than we brought?" Mrs Jenkins exclaims cheerfully. "We've eaten all the food, and drunk all the drink, and yet I'm not sure all of this is going to fit in."

"Ah yes, that's always the way," I smile. "I have no idea why, either, unless you've bought a ton of fudge!"

"Tempting, but we haven't. Christmas is coming, I think there will be treats enough!"

I smile. "I'll be in the Mowhay if you need anything, or else just leave your key in the door when you're done. I hope you have a good journey home."

"Thank you so much, Alice. It's really been a lovely week. Please pass on our thanks to Julie, too. It's been a real touch of luxury, having somebody chef for us, and then getting to eat in the comfort of our own home! Well, holiday home… you know what I mean! Maybe we'll have Christmas here one year."

"Well, just let me know, if you want to book."

"I will. And good luck, with…" she gestures to my obviously pregnant tummy. "You must be shattered."

"I am, a bit, but we're on the home strait now. I've just got to make it through to New Year, then I should have a good couple of weeks at least, before he or she makes their appearance. I'm planning to put my feet up for a bit then."

I head across to the Mowhay, with Ben and Meg

scampering along in front, and I open the bifold doors, although it is a bit chilly. But I'd rather let the outside in whenever I can (at the risk of sounding like I'm on a *Grand Designs* episode).

Lizzie will be here soon, to finalise details of next week's yoga retreat, so I settle Ben at the table with some colouring-in – Christmas print-outs, of a snowman (of course). I really think we should revise these snowy festive images. They are giving children false hope. Maybe some nice grey clouds, and people wearing anoraks, hoods up against the rain – the washing machine on, cleaning a load of muddy clothes. Or a parent at a computer, desperately trying to source this year's sold-out Christmas toy, or pressing 'refresh' on an Amazon Black Friday screen, to grab a bargain. A child having a full-on meltdown because the countdown to Christmas now starts in November, and they just can't cope with the anticipation any longer. These would be more realistic. Not so magical, though, I guess.

❄ ❄ ❄

"Hi, Alice." Lizzie greets me with a warm hug. "You're looking well. But a bit tired," she says on closer inspection. "I hope you're taking some time to rest."

"Of course," I say, starting to feel irritated by everyone's insistence on my resting. I am going to, and soon. Just three weeks' time, and I'm off!

"Good. And sorry, I don't want to annoy you. I know you're more than capable of everything you're doing. You just need to look after yourself."

"I am doing," I tell her, softening at her words. "I promise I am. It's just this time of year is quite hectic. But Christmas should be quite chilled out, at Mum and Dad's."

"Oh yes, that's such a lovely idea. How nice to be a hotel guest!"

"I know! I can't wait."

"Now, what are we doing today? I know we need to talk through the plan for next week but it's such a lovely day, I wondered if we have to do it here, or if you and Ben would like to come to the beach with me? Just for an hour or two," she interjects, quickly. "I know you're busy. But a bit of sea air will do you good. And Ben and Meg can play while we talk."

"OK!" I laugh. She's answered all my objections before I've had a chance to air them. "Actually, Lizzie, that sounds great. Yes please."

"Alright, well I'll drive. I'm going to take you to one of my secret spots. I don't share them with many people, you know."

"Well, this sounds better and better," I smile. I close up the Mowhay doors, while Lizzie goes to find Ben and Meg and shepherd them towards her car.

Cindy arrives on her bike, looking rosy-cheeked and invigorated, just as I'm approaching the car park.

"Morning!" I say. "I'm about to be whisked away to the beach by Lizzie. The guests have all gone, as you can see," I say, gesturing to the car park, which is empty now, aside from my car and Lizzie's. "If you can make a start, I'll be back later this morning and help finish things off."

"You'll do nothing of the sort!" Cindy scolds. "I mean, come back, of course," she flusters a little, as though remembering I'm her manager, although our working relationship quickly became a friendship some time ago and she should know I won't mind her talking to me like that. "What I mean is, you're not to be doing any of the cleaning, you're fit to burst. I'll have it all done, and then you can just have a wander round and make sure everything's as it should be."

Everyone's so kind, when you're pregnant. It's nice to be spoiled a little, I can't deny it. And I quite like people making decisions for me, just for now, while it sometimes feels like I'm too tired to think straight.

I get Ben's car seat from my car. It's heavy and bulky. Everything seems a bit more of an effort these days, somehow. But I try not to show it.

"Well, I don't have any doubt that everything will be brilliant," I smile. "Thank you, Cindy." I rub my lower back. "I am definitely feeling it now, you know."

"I remember it well," Cindy says as she opens one of the back doors of Lizzie's car, for me to slide the seat in. "I think with the second one, your body's a bit more ready for what's about to happen. I remember feeling like James was going to fall out of me at times! If that's not too much information."

"No, I know exactly what you mean! Let's hope that doesn't happen, though. I need this one to stay put for another few weeks! I'll see you in a couple of hours."

Lizzie arrives with Meg and Ben, and she lets Meg in through the hatchback, while I help Ben into his seat. Then I ease myself into Lizzie's passenger seat.

"Off we go, then!" Lizzie smiles. I note the lump of rose quartz tucked into the compartment where most people keep change for car parks. And the car smells lovely – patchouli, I think.

"Where's this mysterious cove, then?" I ask.

"You'll see," she slides a sly smile sideways. "Though maybe I should blindfold you, so you can't find it again! Before I know it, you'll be sending all your Amethi folks down there."

"I won't, I promise!" I laugh.

"Good. I think you're going to love it. You too, Benny!" she glances in the mirror.

Ben falls asleep within minutes.

"Bless him," Lizzie says. "Look up there, Alice."

I follow her gaze, up to some standing stones high up on a rugged hill.

"Think how old they are, Alice. Imagine the people who put them there."

This is a side of Cornwall I have yet to explore, though I often think I must. There are sixteen stone circles in this county, and many more standing stones, monuments and burial chambers. At Chyauster, there is what is thought by some to be the remains of the oldest street in the United Kingdom. Why I haven't made it to any of these places yet is beyond me, but I suppose that, as is often the case when you actually live somewhere, day-to-day life takes over and you forget to really take note of what is right in front of you. I'm sure most Londoners don't spend many days going around the museums, to the West End, and Buckingham Palace. We are all too busy living our lives.

"When this baby's here," I say, rubbing my belly, "I might do a bit of exploring, while Ben's at nursery." I imagine my baby strapped to my front, me striding up hills, over the moors, around the stones. I want to see them, to touch them. Find out if I feel anything, and try to connect even more deeply with this beautiful place. I'm not sure what I'm expecting, or imagining, I might feel, but maybe there is something. The memory contained in the stones. The energy of the people who carried them, and placed them. Then again, maybe that's a load of old claptrap. I want to believe, but I'm also a little cynical – or sceptical, at the very least. I'm open-minded about most things, but

I have no firm beliefs, and I wish I had, in a way.

"I'll come with you, if you like," Lizzie offers. "I can be your tour guide."

While a part of me relishes the idea of some time to myself, just my baby and me, I know that I'd be lost, and less confident, without Lizzie by my side. Plus, she's probably been to these places hundreds of times, and I know she's good at giving space, allowing time for peace. "I'd love that," I say, and I mean it.

The beach, as it turns out, is just twenty minutes away by car. It is not all that far from Paul and Shona's house, which is above another tiny beach, tucked well away from those who don't know the county well. I remember when we were tentatively dating, and Paul had taken me there, unwilling to let on that the large, swanky house in the woods was actually his. Sometimes I can't believe that he and I were so close to being in a relationship. I mean, he really is a lovely person (not to mention incredibly good-looking), but we're at such different points in our lives. I'm closer in age to his kids than to him. And he's loaded. He's made his money, he's had his family. Shona is definitely a better match. I wouldn't say no to his house, though. What a place.

Lizzie pulls the car over into a tiny layby. "No toilets here, I'm afraid," she says, "but there are plenty of trees."

I don't fancy trying to crouch behind a tree in the sloped woodlands. I would be fine getting down, I just don't think I'd be able to get up again. An image springs to mind, of me tumbling head over heel down the earthy slope, trousers round my ankles. Not a very flattering image, I must say, and not a very appealing thought.

"I'd help you if you needed it," Lizzie smiles, as if

reading my mind. "Nothing I haven't seen before."

"Well, I'll try and last till we get back anyway!" I laugh.

I follow Lizzie, tentatively picking my way between the trees, and taking careful steps so as not to slip. It's not horrendously steep, but I can't be too careful. I stop for a moment, to listen to the birdsong, which resounds between the bare branches. Ben and Meg are dashing through the fallen leaves – still dry from the lack of rain.

I breathe. And smile. I needed this.

"You OK, my love?" Lizzie asks.

"I'm fine," I say. "Just taking a moment."

"You do that," she says approvingly.

In time, I begin to walk again and I catch up with the other three, just as we reach a small opening, with some higgledy-piggledy steps created from planks of wood, built up with rocks, beyond which is the beach. It is tiny, and beautiful. The sea is lapping the shore and there is seaweed and driftwood strewn across the sand.

"Wow!"

"I thought you might say that," grins Lizzie.

Ben and Meg run onto the beach, Meg barking and Ben laughing. There are piles of rocks on either side of the sand, stacked up as though they have tumbled down the cliffs. On the south side, back inside the cliff, is a gaping hole.

"Is that a cave?" I ask Lizzie.

"It is. Do you want to have a look?"

"Yes!" I say excitedly, all thoughts of work dissipating into the air. "Ben!" I call. "Meg!" They both come bounding over, Ben's face flushed and Meg's tongue lolling from her mouth. "We're going to explore that cave, Ben. Would you like to come?"

Not that I'm about to leave him out on the beach on his own if he says no.

"Yes!" he shouts. "Can we?"

"Of course!" I laugh, but he's already off, his tiny legs somehow propelling him across the sand at a speed I don't think I could achieve even if I wasn't heavily pregnant. He's so small and so light that he doesn't make an impact.

Lizzie helps me across a couple of the rocks. They're higher than they looked from back at the bottom of the woods. I look behind, and I can barely make out where the entrance is. The woods close in, trees joining forces, like they're linking arms, forbidding passage.

Meg doesn't seem to want to come into the cave. Perhaps it's too dark for her.

"Come on," I say. "Come to me." She sits, very firmly, on the rocks. "Come on, Meg." I try again but she stands, and barks at me. "OK. You stay here. We won't be long."

The air around us turns noticeably colder the moment we step through the mouth of the cave. "It's very dark," I say dubiously, hit by a sudden sense of dread. Ben's hand is very quickly in mine. I squeeze it, comforted by the familiar, warm, soft skin. While my eyes grow accustomed to the light, I look to my left, to Lizzie, who is standing very still.

"There are tunnels there," she says.

"Tunnels?"

"Yes. Two of them. One was used by farmers, collecting seaweed. The other goes to the ullies."

"The…?"

"Ullies. They're used by fishermen, or they were, to keep their catches of shellfish."

"Phew, I thought you were going to say they were smugglers' tunnels."

"Oh, without doubt, they were."

I shiver involuntarily, and listen to the slow, occasional

drip of water from somewhere in the dark recesses of the cave.

"What do you think, Ben?" Lizzie asks.

Ben is very quiet, just staring around him. "Are there bears here?" he whispers.

"No, Ben, I shouldn't think so," I say cheerily, hearing my voice rebound from the cold, damp walls. "Did you hear that echo?" I ask him.

"What's a echo?"

"Oh, it's the sound of something coming back – bouncing off the walls." I start to flounder, thinking, actually, what is an echo? I mean, I know roughly, but could I really explain it, scientifically? Luckily, Ben is two, and at the moment he's young enough to think I know everything. He accepts my poor explanation without further question.

"I want to go out," says Ben. "See Meg."

"OK, my lovely. Let's go." I turn apologetically to Lizzie. "Ben doesn't like it." I'm not sure I do, either, though it's definitely intriguing. I half want to leave, and half want to push on through, explore the tunnels. Find out if they hold anything more than cold, wet seaweed.

"No, he's very sensitive. Meg, too. But then, animals always are."

We emerge gladly into the daylight, the sun just pushing its way through the cloud cover, which seems to have stuck around for days now. I am lifted by the sight of the sparkles splashing across the sea. Far out, a fishing boat passes by.

I think of smugglers, waiting here in this cove, for the boats that would bring in their bounty. Brandy, gin, rum, tobacco. Even tea. That cave, and the tunnels, would be perfect for hiding their stash, and then bringing it up to the higher land, where it might be dispersed, behind the backs, and sometimes even under the noses, of the law-keepers. There would have been some dark deeds associated with some of these people, and I can't deny I am relieved to be out here. My breathing is easier, somehow.

"Is it… haunted?" I ask Lizzie.

"The cave?" Lizzie asks.

"Yes. The cave, the tunnels. The beach. It is beautiful here, but I feel a bit weird."

"There are a few stories, but there are everywhere, aren't there?" Lizzie laughs, slightly uneasily, I think.

"Yes, that's true. What do they say about this place, though?"

"Well, I don't know. Maybe I shouldn't say. Given your…" she eyes the mound of my belly.

"No, go on," I say. "I don't mind."

"OK. Well, I first heard about this place years ago. And I know a couple of stories about it. One's about a young woman, who was on a boat that got into difficulty just out there, where the bay opens out and the sea's wilder. The lifeboat came, and the woman survived, but she had a baby with her. Rose. And the baby was swept away. Swallowed by the waves. Elizabeth Grayley – that was the mother's name – lived to quite an age, they say, but she never got over the loss of her child. At her funeral, some say her spirit left the grave, and moved away towards the sea. On stormy nights, she's been seen on this beach, here, looking out to sea, searching for Rose. Other nights, when it's quiet and still, you might hear her crying. Some say they've seen a female figure on the rocks. Hunched in on herself, in distress. But when they approach, she vanishes."

"That's so sad," I say. "And she was Elizabeth, like you."

"Aye," Lizzie's eyes are on the waves, as if searching for this child herself. "Heartbreaking."

32

"You said there are a couple of stories?" I prompt, wanting to move on from this tale, which is a little too close to the bone for my liking. My imagination can go into overdrive sometimes, when it comes to bad things happening to babies and children.

"That's right," Lizzie turns back to me. "Well, you know you mentioned smugglers…"

"Yes?"

"Legend has it that there were two rival gangs in this part of the county, for quite some time. Probably more than two, I should think, but this story relates particularly to two fearsome crews, who each wanted this patch for themselves. They harangued the local villages and travellers, and cast fear into the hearts of landowners."

"You're good at this story-telling," I say to Lizzie, trying to smile, but somehow not quite able to shake off the chill from the cave, and the story of Elizabeth and Rose.

"One night, one of the gangs was expecting a delivery, if you know what I mean. They were waiting here, on this very beach, hidden in the shadows of the rocks. They were meant to flash lantern lights, to alert the boat to their whereabouts, but had to be very careful not to catch anyone else's attention. Unknown to them, the other lot were tucked away just round there, on the rocks." She gestures to an outcrop sticking well out into the sea. "They knew the tactics, and they used their own lights, to catch the boat crew's attention, and divert them from course. The boat crashed and wrecked on the rocks, and the rival gang got most of the cargo, before the other lot could get to them. Did you know, the law in those days stated that it was illegal to salvage anything from a ship that was wrecked but had any living people on it? It seems ridiculous now; it was basically condemning any crew or passengers on a wrecked boat to death. Anyway, on this particular night, as the story goes, the men here on the beach heard the sound of the crash, and the cries of the men from the boat, as they fell in and drowned or, more likely, were slain by the rival gang. Those on the beach couldn't get to them in time to help. Since then, they say, on a quiet night you can hear the sound of that boat crashing on the rocks, and the men perishing in the sea. And some say they've seen a boat land on this beach in the dead of night, and a boat load of men disembark onto the sand, then the whole lot of them vanish into nothing."

So, on a quiet night, you can hear the woman crying, *and* the boat load of men arriving on the sand, I think, welcoming in my cynicism like an old friend. I wonder if they bother each other. Glad as I am to be able to laugh at the idea of these ghosts, there is a little part of me that wonders if there could be any truth in the stories.

"Have you witnessed any of this yourself?" I ask Lizzie, trying not to sound like I don't believe her. My eyes are on Ben, now sitting in the sand next to Meg, who is rapidly digging a hole. Ben is laughing, and throwing sand into the air. I'm glad to have such a wholesome, innocent sight to focus on.

"The smugglers? No, no. And I've not been here at night for a long time, though I often mean to."

"You're a braver woman than me!" I laugh. I'm glad Lizzie waited till after we were in the cave, to tell me about all this. Out here, sunshine is spilling onto the sand, and the waves rolling in are gentle, just frothing slightly as they shyly hit the shore.

"It's fantastic during the day!" Lizzie says. "There is rarely another soul around. Well, not ones we can see anyway!" she laughs, and I smile back, but my imagination has been caught, and I think there is a part of me that would like to come here at night. But I know I'd never dare.

"There's another story about this little beach," Lizzie says. "That these piles of rocks and boulders were dumped here by a giant emptying his pockets." I do laugh out loud now. This seems like safer ground. Even Lizzie can't believe in giants – can she? "Anyway," she continues, "we'd better make sure we do actually talk work before we go back, seeing as that was what we came to do."

5

In the evening, I relay Lizzie's stories to Sam.

"Oh yeah," he says with a grin. "Cornwall's certainly got its share of ghosts. Or stories, I should say."

"You don't believe?"

"Nah!" he smiles, putting his arm around me. "I don't reckon. And they say a lot of the ghost stories were made up by the smugglers themselves, to keep nosy locals away from their dodgy dealings. There's some castle somewhere, though I don't think it's Cornwall, where there used to be sightings of a White Lady, whenever a shipment of illicit booze was due in. One of the gang, using phosphorous to make themselves glow! No, can't say I believe in any of that," he says definitely.

Although I was happy to doubt, I'm disappointed, somehow, that Sam is so immovable in his disbelief. "Do you not think the existence of ghosts is even a possibility?"

"I don't know," he looks thoughtful. "Doesn't make much sense to me. I'm too scientific, maybe."

"So, you think science explains everything?"

"Well… yeah. There's always a rational explanation."

"What about the solstice celebrations? Don't you feel anything then?"

"I do," he concedes, "but I'd say that's down to human spirit and us all being together. Like a group emotion."

"Is that scientific?"

"Not especially!" he laughs. "But ghosts… I don't think so. No, this is it," he says firmly. "When you're gone, you're gone."

"But where to? Where does all our energy go?" I press.

"I don't know!" he laughs again. "God, I'm going to have to ban you from spending time with Lizzie if this is the kind of stuff you come back with. Now, are we going to watch this film or not?"

I snuggle into his warmth, and predictably I am asleep before half an hour is up. Sam gently wakes me. "Up to bed with you, Alice."

"What? I'm not asleep," I say indignantly.

"Your snoring says otherwise."

"I don't snore!"

"You keep telling yourself that, my love."

I kneel down to give Meg a rub before I go upstairs, then have to heave myself up onto my feet. Cindy's not wrong about how different a second pregnancy is. It feels like my body's giving up on me. As long as it keeps this baby safe, and delivers it safely... I can concentrate on getting back to some kind of fitness for my own sake later.

I trudge up the stairs, and check in on Ben, whose room is lit with the glow of a thousand stars, from this lovely light that Karen bought for him. It plays music while he's going to sleep, then continues to project stars across the room all night, so that if Ben wakes, he knows he's safe in his own little universe, and it's still time for bed.

I kiss his warm cheek tenderly, and pull his duvet back over him, although I know it will be on the floor again in minutes. He is snoring, too, though I suspect his snores are a little cuter than mine. I have been known to wake myself up with the noise I make, and it's only got worse since I was pregnant.

Then I go into our room, through to the en suite, brush my teeth and wash my face, then back into the cosiness of our bedroom, and lower myself gently into bed. I am looking forward to this sleep. The fresh air from the trip to the beach has made me that special kind of tired, which I love most of all. Exhilarated and exhausted, all at once.

There is no point even pretending I'll get any reading done. I switch off the light and lie still, letting the darkness surround me, and listening to the sounds of the house. I can just hear the muffled music and voices of the film, and the steady whirr of the boiler in the airing cupboard, though the heating should go off soon. While the days are still relatively warm, the nights are turning colder, which is a relief. I don't think I could bear those warm, sticky summer nights, the way I feel right now. I close my eyes, and place my hand on my tummy. As ever, I feel an answering kick – or a nudge. Maybe this baby's going to be a real livewire, or perhaps it's just trying to get me to leave it alone. *This is my space.*

It does feel like that, sometimes, with pregnancy, and motherhood. You are giving yourself over, almost entirely, for the sake of another (or others). First with pregnancy – invaded by an interloper, no matter how welcome, your muscles stretch to make way (one of my excuses for why my snoring has got so much worse), your back might ache, feet swell, all the goodness and nutrients from your food passed on to this little alien growing inside you. Then the birth. Let's just say – ow. And then, looking after a baby. You are in thrall to their feeding schedule, and changing, and sleeping, and cuddling, and entertaining, and soothing, and comforting. It is impossible to imagine, until you experience it first-hand, how your life is completely and utterly all about them and their needs.

As the child grows, some of these things are no longer required, but you can bet there are plenty more demands on you, ready to muscle in. Ben is only two, but I have heard other mothers, with older children, talking about how much we are still needed, even when our children are teenagers – maybe needed more than ever. Grown-up social lives put on hold, or at least majorly dampened down, to make way for our offspring's. Ferrying around to parties, or classes and clubs; school trips; pocket money; expensive technology. But more importantly, being aware and being there, and trying to guide them through the process of growing up. Even if we realise now that parents are still growing up themselves. Still learning. It's the ultimate exercise in altruism. Only it isn't all altruism, is it? For many of us, hopefully most of us, we want all this. Many women have waited years, known since they were children, that they wanted to be mothers themselves. And while our days become ruled by these tiny emperors, and sometimes we're in tears – of stress, anxiety, confusion, love, or, let's be honest, boredom – we know it's all worth it, and it's not all about the baby. It's about us, and our maternal needs, or wants.

I am keenly aware of this, and all the more so while Julie, for whatever reason (or more likely for no reason but pure bad luck) has not been able to get pregnant. She and Luke have adopted their daughter Zinnia, and I know Julie tries not to look back. I certainly know that her love for Zinnie is as fierce and true as mine is for Ben.

Then there is David, who, along with his husband Martin, adopted two tiny children. David put his career on hold to become a dad. So I know it's not just mums. I do, really. But there are some immediate, physical maternal demands, which men will never feel. It's a simple, immovable, biological fact.

I move my hand to my own heart. I've been experiencing some palpitations lately, and I do know that when other people tell me to slow down, they're right. But the end is in sight, and I know what I'm doing. Just a few weeks now, and I can do as they advise. Put my feet up and enjoy a little time to myself, while Ben is at nursery or with Karen, before the new one comes and starts to rule the roost. How will Ben take to his new role? What will he think of his little brother or sister? Will he feel usurped? What if I don't love the new baby as much as I love Ben? It is difficult imagining loving anybody else so much but, again, those that have gone before me reassure me that I will be amazed to find I have so much more love to give, and just as much for my second child as my first.

Stop it, I tell myself. *You're meant to be going to sleep.* I've managed to fill my head with thoughts and worries which, unless I am very careful, will continue to go round and round inside my mind. I had fallen asleep a very short way into a film and now, in the dark, in my cosy, warm bed, I am wide awake. I plump up my pillows, and lie back and close my eyes. *Just breathe*, I think, channelling Lizzie.

Nevertheless, sleep takes a long time to come, but come it must have, because the next thing I know, I'm sitting up sharply, shocked suddenly from my sleep, my heart beating ten to the dozen, and Sam breathing deeply next to me.

Ben, Ben, Ben, I am thinking, and I get out of bed, push my way through the darkness, into the hallway, and into our little boy's room. There he is, lying in the glow of his stars. Breathing deeply. Safe and sound.

I hear Meg stir downstairs and I decide to go down and see her. Maybe make myself a drink. What made me wake like that? I pat Meg, who looks puzzled but pleased to see me at this time of night, and I go into the kitchen, getting a pan down to warm some milk. I know I could use the microwave, but there is something soothing about doing it this way, and the smell of the milk as it begins to heat.

I turn my mind back, trying to recall my dream, and pinpoint what scared me. *The sea*, I think. Something to do with the sea. Lizzie's stories spring to mind, and I wonder if I've been dreaming about them. Elizabeth Grayley and her baby, Rose. What an unimaginably awful thing to happen. And, though I don't think I believe the ghost story – a spirit rising from the grave and floating out to sea is a bit farfetched for me, no matter how open-minded I like to think I am – the thought of that baby drowning, separated from her desperate mother, has touched a nerve. It has maybe also tapped into the feelings I've sometimes tried to avoid when I've watched the news on TV and been brought stories of refugees drowning in their bid to cross the channel. Adults, teenagers, children, toddlers, babies.

It's all mixed up in my mind. It's just horrendous. Maybe because I love the sea so, and yet I can see its sinister potential; can imagine the terror and panic of a rough journey, in a tiny boat.

Stop it, I tell myself, dipping my little finger into the milk to test the temperature. *This is not going to help you get back to sleep, Alice.*

The kitchen blinds are open, as they always are. None of our neighbours can see in, and so the blinds stay gathered up, collecting dust. In the summer, I like to see the morning sunshine flooding in, but with the inside light on now, the outside world looks pitch-black. When I was little, I would have hated that. The thought that there might be somebody outside who I couldn't see, but who could see me.

Great. Now I've got that in my head, too! I might just shut those blinds, after all. I turn the hob off, and feel

Meg's nose against my leg. I put my hand down behind me to stroke her. She's not there. I turn and she is at the kitchen doorway, looking not at me, but past me, her hackles up, and a low growl in her throat.

"Meg? What is it? What is it, girl?"

She doesn't move her eyes towards me, then she's crouching low, then up on her toes, and barking, like when she's spotted a squirrel in a tree.

"Meg! Stop it!" I hiss. "You'll wake the others up."

She's barking again, and now I'm on edge. I really wish the blinds were closed.

"Alice? Are you OK?" I hear Sam's worried voice, and his footsteps hurrying down the stairs. It seems to break Meg's spell, and she goes to him, but she's clearly still agitated.

"I'm fine. I just couldn't sleep, so I decided to make a drink." I do feel ever so slightly shaky. "Something just set Meg off, that's all."

"I'll check outside," Sam says, and he switches on the outside light, which illuminates the garden, and I can see it is empty. Why didn't I think to do that? Opening the back door, Sam ushers Meg outside. "Go on, girl," he says, and follows her.

I decide to add some hot chocolate powder to the milk. Maybe a bit of sugar will settle my nerves a little. Sam is soon back in. "It's cold out," he says, "but there's nothing there. Must have been a fox or something."

"That's probably it," I say, as he calls Meg back in and sends her back to her bed. She trots off obediently, as though nothing has happened.

"Come on, Alice," Sam says. "Bring that back to bed. It's too cold to be down here. Why don't you read for a bit? You'll soon drop off."

"Alright." Glad of his company, I follow him to our room, popping in to look at Ben again on the way, and retrieving his duvet from the floor once more.

Sam is already in bed, not quite asleep, when I get to our doorway. I envy him his ability to drop off like this. Before I close the door, I go to switch off the downstairs lights, but I think that actually, just tonight, I will leave them on.

6

"Oh you're having weird hormonal dreams," Sandi, the midwife, says to me at my check-up. "That is very common, at this stage of pregnancy. And unsettled nights. It's just typical, isn't it? Right when we need our sleep, our bodies and hormones decide to mess us around. Some people think it's Mother Nature trying to prepare women for unsettled nights ahead, when the baby needs feeding. Between you and me, I think that's bollocks."

I laugh. It makes me feel better. And now I think of it, I do remember having strange dreams when I was pregnant with Ben. See what I mean, about pregnancy taking us over? Not just our bodies, but our minds, too.

"OK, everything feels like it's as it should be with baby, it feels like it might already have engaged," she says, pressing around my tummy firmly. "That's very good for a second baby. I'm sure that's its bottom right there. Lovely. Let's hope it's a well-behaved one, eh? And now, my love, it's your turn. Can't forget mums, can we? You're very important people."

"I'm glad you think so," I smile. "I remember when I had Ben, while I was pregnant everyone made a fuss of me, then after he was born, it felt like that was it, as far as I was concerned. I don't mean Sam, of course," I hasten to add, "but out and about. Suddenly, it's all about the baby. Well, I suppose it always was, really, but you do feel sometimes like you're overlooked, once the baby's born."

"You're absolutely right, lovey, and that's why it's really important to check in with us, or the health visitor. We are just as bothered about you as your baby. And if you have any problems, feel low, just tell us. Don't suffer in silence."

"I won't. I promise." I pull up my sleeve so she can fit the blood pressure cuff around my arm. She watches the numbers on the screen.

"A little bit high there, Alice. Not horrendously, and it's perfectly normal for it to start to pick up a bit at this stage. After all, you've got a lot of extra blood to pump around your body now. Look," She turns the screen so I can see. "That top number is the systolic reading, the pressure as your heart pushes the blood around, and the bottom one is the diastolic number, which is when your heart relaxes in between beats... These are just within what we consider a healthy range," Sandi says, "but we don't really want them to go any higher. Now, when are you stopping work?"

"New Year." I feel like my heart is beating faster at this conversation. I know about high blood pressure in pregnancy, and pre-eclampsia.

"OK. Well, what I'd like you to do is come back next week, so we can just keep an eye on you. And if you feel faint, or ill in any way, give me a call, OK?"

"What happens if it goes higher?"

"If it goes higher, and it is an if," she says gently, "then depending on how high, we can keep checking you daily. And if it will give you peace of mind, you can get your own monitor, from the chemist, or buy one online. If it went up to a stage where I thought it might be a problem, then I'd say you should be in hospital to be monitored."

"I can't do that!" I blurt out. "I've got Ben, and work. We've got solstice week, and Christmas, and New Year."

"Alice," she says, putting her hand on my arm. "I said *if*. But you must know that we have to do what's best for the baby, and you, and if your blood pressure should rocket up, then we'll have to go down that route. However, we are not there now, and we hopefully won't be. The best thing you can do is keep active – but not too active – and eat well. And make time to unwind, too. And try not to worry, OK? That's not good for blood pressure!"

It's hard not to worry when you've just said I might have to go to hospital, I huff inwardly, but just say, "OK."

"We're just making sure you and baby keep well," Sandi says. "And I promise it is about you and not just the baby, OK? You are just as important."

"Thank you," I smile. I know it's not her fault, and she is just doing her job, and what's more, doing it to the best of her abilities. I know I am in safe hands. It's just that a spell in hospital is not part of the plan.

"Life doesn't always go according to plan," she says, as if reading my mind. "But it's good that you've only got three more weeks of work to go. You make the most of that time when you're off, OK? Before baby comes."

"I will."

I really will, I tell myself. I will have a walk each day, and then lots of time watching TV. Get some box sets lined up... I remember when I was at school, if I had to have a day or two off ill, lying on the settee with a duvet over me, watching inane daytime TV. When was the last time I lay on the settee for hours, watching rubbish? Or even watching something good? I can't remember. Most of the TV I watch at the moment seems to be *Ben and Holly*, or CBeebies. By the time Ben's asleep, and I might be able to watch something I like, alone or with Sam, more often than not I am so tired that I just fall asleep as soon as I've relaxed. I promise myself a bit of time to just slob about and watch TV – no guilt – and to truly, one hundred per cent, relax, before baby number two makes an appearance.

And maybe I will get one of those monitors for myself, too. Just so I can be sure I'm OK. As long as I don't get obsessive, and start checking myself every ten minutes.

❄ ❄ ❄

In the afternoon, Julie and I are both away from Amethi, as it's Goslings Nursery's Christmas Play. It sounds very grand, but Angie has warned us not to expect too much.

"It's not going to be like you see on TV," she says. "But the children are very excited, and really looking forward to showing their mummies and daddies what they've been learning."

Sam can't make it, unfortunately, and neither can Luke. And looking around the audience, I can see it is mostly made up of mums, and grandparents, with the odd dad dotted here and there. This is not necessarily a reflection on dads themselves, but on their place in the world. Could they really ask to take time off work for their two-year-old's Christmas play? Would such a request be looked on with scorn? For Sam's part, he has been booked in for months to give a talk at a local business network's Christmas lunch – about conservation in general, and in particular locally, hoping to get businesses on board with a beach-cleaning project, the idea being that employees are given an afternoon every two months to take time out on the beach, helping to keep it litter-free. The benefits to the businesses are: employees being given a bit of headspace (yes, they might be picking up other people's litter, but they are doing it on a beach, by the sea, and out of the office for a change of scene – and getting paid for it!); fulfilling social responsibility obligations, and also, with so many local businesses being tied up with tourism, helping to make

Cornwall the best it can be, and therefore more attractive to tourists. It's a win-win.

"I've got to try and make this bloody talk funny, though," Sam lamented to me. "They'll all be pissed, it's their Christmas lunch. I've got to keep their attention."

"Good luck with that! But at least if they're pissed, there's more chance of them signing up."

"True."

Anyway, that is why Sam isn't here. Luke is back in London, where he spends a lot less time these days, but he's also at a Christmas lunch, with one of his clients.

"Why aren't we having a Christmas lunch?" I asked Julie when she told me. "We never do."

"No, we just provide everyone else's!"

Now, she and I squeeze into seats at the end of the row – me at the very end, so I have a little extra space. I am not the only pregnant woman in the room, and a couple of us smile knowingly, and sympathetically at each other as we wedge ourselves into the small, child-sized seats. I just hope mine doesn't give way.

We are in the large room, where the older children are normally based. There is a hush, as the door to the adjoining room opens and the children are ushered in. Mary is a tall (for a three-year-old) girl I recognise as she lives further down our road, while the boy playing Joseph is a good few inches shorter than her. He stops and waves at his mum. Everyone says, "Aaahhhh." The nursery staff bring the children in and settle them in rows in front of us. It's actually really hard to see them, as they're sitting cross-legged on the floor, but they are brought to stand up in groups. Ben is a shepherd, and Zinnie a star. The nativity story is told in a very short and sweet way, and the children then all stand and sing a jaunty little number about the

48

wise men following the star. Halfway through, a little boy begins to cry, and is carried away into his grandma's waiting arms. The others stand and sing shyly, into their chests, or loud and proud, heads held high, swinging side-to-side. None of them can stand still. There is pulling of costumes – sometimes their own, sometimes another child's – and swaying around, while they sing or chant the words along with the smiling staff . Out of time and out of tune, but just incredibly sweet.

"Are you crying?" Julie leans towards me.

"No," I say, blowing my nose surreptitiously.

"Nor me," she says, wiping her eyes.

We both laugh quietly.

Afterwards, there are mince pies and cups of tea for the grown-ups, and the children cling to us, proud of themselves for performing in their first Christmas play.

"Go on, you two, go and play," I say. Once the children are out of sight and I have made sure there are no gossipy types in earshot, I tell Julie, "I've got high blood pressure."

Her face falls.

"Not terribly high," I add. "Not enough to floor me, but it is close."

"Oh no, Alice, I'm sorry," she says. "Are you OK? What can we do?"

The 'we' makes me smile. I love this woman.

"Nothing, really, at the moment. Just keep an eye on it. I go back in a week to have it checked again."

"What did Sam say?"

"I haven't told him," I confess.

"Alice! You can't not tell him. He needs to know."

"But he might want me to stop work early."

"He might. But he might not. But do you think you

should?" she asks, earnestly.

"No! No, no. Sandi said it's not too bad, and she'd have said if it was. No, I just need to be careful."

"Even so, Alice. Think about it. We'll manage, you know. I don't mean we don't need you… but we are going to have to do without you for a while next year."

"Well, yes, but January we're closed, and then it will be quiet till Easter. And by then I might be in a better position to get involved – even if I end up doing the office work at home."

We still haven't really got a plan in place. I think we are just going to have to wing it. I envisage working at home mostly, and just popping up to Amethi when necessary. On Saturdays, which are generally changeover days, Sam will be at home, and he can look after Ben and the baby.

It's messy, I know. But we can't afford to take on anyone else, and besides, it would almost be more work, trying to get someone trained up. No. Between us, we will manage. We're going to have to.

"I'm not missing solstice, or Christmas, or New Year," I say firmly.

"Well, let's play it by ear, shall we? If you're not well, you need to say."

"I promise I will."

She looks at me.

"I promise!" I laugh.

We make our excuses after about ten minutes, and head home, the children delighted to be leaving nursery a little earlier than usual, and still buoyed up from their performance on stage.

As we walk along our street, I can see that Sam has just arrived home. He turns and smiles at the sound of our voices.

"Daddy!" Ben cries, and runs ahead, to be scooped up and swung into the air.

"How was the play, Benny?"

"Brilliant!" Ben shouts.

I smile. "It was lovely."

"Did you cry?"

"Might have."

"I knew it!"

"So how was your speech?" I ask.

"It was good! Really good. Steve's pleased, cos we've got eight sign-ups to the project."

"That's brilliant! And did you get any laughs?"

"Not really," he admits. "I decided against that tactic. I just talked to them about the impact of litter in the oceans, and the positive impact that volunteering's having, in keeping Cornwall clean, and on the volunteers themselves. Also on a company's credentials, if they can claim to be working in the spirit of social responsibility."

"Sounds like it went very well!" I say, kissing him.

"And how was your day? Apart from the play, I mean. Everything alright with the midwife?"

"Great," I say airily. "The baby's growing well, but not too much. And it might even have engaged already, the clever little blighter. I got to listen to the heartbeat, which you know I love. And I'm OK, but my blood pressure's just a teeny bit high." I rush these last words out, as if hoping he won't hear them. But Julie is right, I couldn't not tell Sam about this.

"What?" he says, immediately concerned. "Are you alright, Alice?"

"Yes, I am. It's within the right parameters. I just need to keep an eye on it. And eat well. And be active."

"But not too active," he says.

"Exactly."

"I know you don't want me to play the over-protective husband. And you're right in the middle of everything with work. But I wouldn't be a very good husband, if I didn't say anything. You need to put yourself first."

"And the baby?" I say, unjustly irritated. Sam is not the overbearing type, at all. He knows I love my work, and he loves the fact that I do.

"Well, yes. And the baby. Alice," he says, before I can reply. "I know, it's your body, your pregnancy. But it is kind of mine, too. The pregnancy, or at least the baby. Sorry. This isn't coming out right. Your body's your body, but the baby is yours and mine. If I could do some of this pregnancy for you, I would. But I can't. But I love you, and I love Ben, and I love this new little one, even though I haven't met it yet. It's not fair, I know it's not, that you're bearing the brunt of it, but there is literally nothing I can do about that. Except to try and look after you, and make sure you stay well."

"I know," I sigh. "I do know all of that. And I won't put work before my health, or the baby's. Of course I won't. I will be careful."

"And you'll let me know if you don't feel well?"

"I will let you know."

"Alright." He kisses the top of my head, lingering just for a moment. I know he'll be worried, and I am too, if I'm honest, but I will take my lead from Sandi, and for now just carry on, being a little more careful and aware than before. "Tell you what," he says, "I know we were going to wait till the weekend, but why don't I take Ben out now, to get the Christmas tree? And you can have a bit of a chill. Why don't you run a bath? Not too hot, mind."

I smile at this, and so does he. He knows I know, but

can't help himself.

"I'll pick up something nice to eat as well," he finishes, watching my face for approval.

"That sounds lovely," I say. "I'm supposed to be eating healthily, though. And keeping the salt intake down."

"Alright, why don't I just do us some pasta when we get back? Then I'll put the tree up after Ben's gone to bed, and we can decorate it tomorrow."

"That sounds perfect. Thank you, Sam." I hug him, feeling the very definite, solid bulk of my pregnancy between us.

"No problem," he murmurs, holding me tight. "Now get some rest, and we'll get out of here. Ben!"

Ben comes running. Meg comes running, too.

"Sorry, Meg," Sam says. "You're not invited. You stay here with Alice."

We stand in the hallway, watching my husband and son get ready to go, Ben giggling as Sam pretends to get his head stuck in the sleeve of his coat. I am overwhelmed by a rush of love for them both.

It's very quiet, all of a sudden, once they've gone. I turn towards the kitchen, to make a cup of herbal tea. I'll take it upstairs with me to the bath. It's getting dark already, and remembering last night, I close the kitchen blinds, letting the dust fall to the work surfaces.

I wipe them clean while the water boils in the kettle, and realise I am ever so slightly on edge. What if Meg starts barking again? I check the back door is locked, and pour the water into the mug, inhaling the aroma of raspberry leaf that glides up on the steam.

Deep breaths, I tell myself. Something just spooked Meg last night, and maybe it was my fault. Perhaps she could sense my own nervous energy. Nevertheless, I go round the house, closing all the curtains, while the bath is running, before I finally strip off my clothes, and sink gratefully into the not-too-hot water, coating myself in bubbles.

7

For all my bravado, I am worried by this development in my health. I do not want high blood pressure. I don't want to damage my health, or my baby's. And I need to be here for Ben. I can't bear imagining how he would be, if something should happen to me. What sense would he make of it? And would he just forget me, over time? Which would probably be better for him, but is a gut-wrenching thought for me.

I know all of this is counter-productive, creating unnecessary stress for myself. Worrying about things which will hopefully not happen. But I do feel vulnerable in this pregnancy. And aware more than I used to be of how it is not always straightforward, and how giving birth can be a risky business. But I am pretty sure stress is not a helpful factor in lowering blood pressure, and so all this worry might exacerbate the problem, increasing the risk of me being ill.

What is also not all that helpful is that the story Lizzie told me has wormed its way into my mind, and hooked itself there. Not the smugglers, of course. They made their own trouble, and probably deserved all they got. Not the giant, either, though I do like the tales of giants around these parts. Legend has it that a petrified giant's heart is contained in the path up St Michael's Mount – you can see the heart shaped stone quite clearly. But no, it's the woman who lost her baby, who keeps drifting into my mind. When I was falling asleep last night, I had one of those semi-awake dreams, that I was at sea, with a baby, on a tiny boat, with waves reaching up and over the sides. Trying to grab me. Trying to grab my baby. I held her close, and I woke with a jolt at the very moment that the waves were about to win. I was sweating and anxious, and Sam, who had still been awake, sitting reading his book, was looking at me. "Are you OK?" he'd asked, concerned.

"Oh, yeah, just one of those weird flying-floating dreams, you know like you have when you're just falling asleep sometimes," I'd gabbled, not wanting to tell him the truth, for some reason.

He had smiled. "Maybe it'll help if I switch the light off." He laid down his book and kissed me, and then reached across to his lamp. The room was in darkness, and Sam was soon out like his light, but I was awake for some time. The occasional car passing the house, or the end of the road, was a comfort somehow, like I wasn't alone in the world. And, bit by bit, I convinced myself to think of happy things. A day on the beach. A walk on the moors. Christmas morning, with Ben finding his stocking stuffed with small, rustling parcels. I fell asleep at some point, and thankfully had no more dreams, or none that I remember.

However, that first, unhappy dream has stuck somehow, and my mind keeps turning to the poor woman who still looks for her baby. I don't know that I really believe that, of course, and I know I'm following unhealthy lines of thought here, but I can't seem to help it, somehow.

In the office at work, I found myself googling her.

Elizabeth Grayley

I come up with a host of professional profiles, on LinkedIn, but nothing about the woman I'm looking for. I add 'Cornwall' – and 'Ghost', then 'Ghost Story'. There is nothing that relates to the story Lizzie told me. But then, I don't suppose that a ghost would be writing her own Wikipedia entry. There are a few old photos, one of which is of an old lady, in black, with a shawl around her shoulders. Her blue eyes look pale and watery, fixed steadily on the camera. She is not smiling, but then people didn't, in photos, in those days. Could this be the Elizabeth I'm looking for? I feel like I should know, somehow. As though I should have a feeling either way. Maybe I'll ask Lizzie where she heard the story. But then she might think I am becoming obsessed. Maybe I am. I hope not.

I do find myself wondering about her though, this young woman. She lived in a time when people had large families, and often one or two children might be expected to die, which is unimaginably awful. Maybe it would be childhood illnesses and/or malnutrition. Lack of knowledge, or lack of money for medical care. There were extremes of poverty – there still are – but no National Health Service back then, of course. And I can't believe it can have been any less painful, to have a child die, just because you had more of them, or because it might be half-expected. The norm. A child is a child, and it can't be that these days we love our children more than Victorian parents loved theirs.

What was Elizabeth's story, I wonder. Was she poor? Wealthy? Why was she on that boat, anyway? Where was she going? Was she travelling towards something, or trying to leave something behind? And how old was poor little Rose? Was there a husband and father in the picture? Other children? Losing a child to the sea... maybe Rose would have gone on to live a long, full and happy life. Perhaps Elizabeth never stopped blaming herself. But maybe there is such a thing as fate, and this was always how little Rose's life was going to turn out.

I've even thought I'd like to write her story. Make Rose immortal, at least in terms of the printed page. Her life may have been short, but it does not mean she matters less. But really, when would I have the time to write a story? For goodness' sake! I give myself a mental shake. And why this story, in particular? I just know that something about it has touched something deep inside of me. I don't know if I'm in the clutches of hormones, or trying to avoid thinking about my own health. Probably both. I need to get a grip.

Luckily, there is much to keep me occupied. Aside from work, there are Christmas parties to attend. This weekend, Mum and Dad are hosting a 'Sail Loft Soiree', and on Sunday it is the Harbour Hotel do, to which Lydia has invited me, Julie, Sam and Luke. It's going to be very posh. I don't think I've even got a dress I can squeeze into. We'll see.

I tell Jon about it when he calls. Now he and Janie are in Spain, he seems so happy and content with life. It feels unbelievable to me that in the space of a few months, he has completely turned himself around. It's something to remember, I think, in a time when I might feel despair, as surely must happen at some time in my life. So far, I've had brushes with it, but somehow managed to pass it by. Keep bouncing along, so that even if I drag along the bottom from time to time, I always bob back up.

Jon was very close to sinking, last summer, but he's pulled himself around. Counselling has helped, and just being open about things. I hope it's long-term, but at least now Janie knows about it, he will share how he feels with her. Get things out in the open. I've said it before, and I have no doubt I will say it again: the things which go unsaid are often a problem for the very reason that they are unsaid. Misunderstandings arise. Resentment. Unhappiness. And yet, I know this, but still don't always heed it. After all, I was not going to mention my high blood pressure to Sam. Which would have meant covering it up, and worrying even more – and maybe being stressed at home, knocking on how I behave towards him and Ben. Instead, I told him, and he leapt into action, without making a fuss (which is fine by me), but he really looked after me last night, and has vowed to carry on doing so, until I have the baby, and beyond.

"I could get used to this," I said, as he brought me tea on a tray to have in front of the TV, having brought back the Christmas tree, and done Ben's tea, bath and bed.

"Well, you can. For now," he said teasingly. "It is finite, you know. But really, I want to look after you. While you need it. Like you looked after me when I was recovering."

"You're still recovering," I said sternly. He did look tired.

"Yes, I know, but I'm so much better now. Honestly, Alice. And you helped me rest. You *made* me rest! Now it's my turn to do the same for you."

When I went to take my tray to the kitchen, he stopped me. "No, you just stay there," he said.

"Well, if you insist…"

"I do."

So, lucky me. Do I have the perfect man? No, because there is no such thing (no perfect woman, either), but he's pretty bloody good. When I stop and think about how all of this has grown from a short holiday romance, when I

59

was eighteen, I can't help but find it incredible. And the ten years I spent without him, when I thought he'd just given up on me. I never really forgot him. I remember I used to dream about him, sometimes, even years after that summer we met was long gone. And eventually, I found him again. I didn't have to look far. He was right here, where I'd left him, and it turned out he hadn't forgotten me, either. Fate? Maybe. But it's been hard work, too, sometimes.

I realise I'm smiling, as I dawdle my way through my email inbox, my search for Elizabeth Grayley forgotten for now.

"You soppy bugger," I mutter to myself, but it doesn't stop me smiling.

I decide to cut the day short, when I've answered all my emails, and sent joining information to the participants of the upcoming yoga retreat.

I am just sending out the last one when I hear Julie on the stairs up to the office. I hadn't even noticed her arriving.

"Hello!" I call. "You're early!"

No reply.

"Ju-lie!" I call.

Nothing.

I get up and open the office door, looking down onto an empty staircase. A tiny shiver runs along the length of my back, as though somebody is trailing their fingers up it.

"Julie?" I go downstairs. Maybe she turned back and went into the kitchen. But I push open the kitchen door and the room is empty and dark.

Heart beating rapidly, while I tell myself I am being ridiculous, I go quickly back up the stairs and shut my laptop, unplugging it, and pushing it none-too-carefully into my bag.

I hurry back down the stairs and into the open air. It is ever so slightly cooler than it has been, and can almost pass as winter now. Above, a pair of buzzards circle each other, in a wide, sweeping dance, their calls shrill in the quiet sky. The jackdaws in the line of trees rise, bickering, into the air. Talk about atmospheric. But now I'm in the broad daylight, the fear that had built up has just as quickly dissipated.

I hear the jingle of a collar and Meg appears at my side. "Hello, girl," I say, rubbing the top of her head, and her ears. I shut and lock the door behind me, and walk to the car. Julie's is nowhere to be seen – just one of the holiday-makers', and mine, parked opposite it. I must have imagined those footsteps on the stairs. It's the most likely – in fact the only – explanation. A rational explanation. If imagination is rational.

Nevertheless, once I'm safely in the car and heading steadily along the drive, I can't help checking my mirror. Just to make sure there is nobody back there watching me.

8

"We don't have to do any of this," Sam says. "You're busy enough, Alice."

"You're just trying to get out of the parties!" I laugh.

"That's as maybe," I notice he doesn't deny it, "but you're going to do yourself in, going from Amethi to your mum and dad's, to the Harbour the next day."

It's the Harbour Hotel one he really doesn't want to do, and he has said as much, but I feel like we need to support Lydia, and I am also unashamedly nosy. After the worries I had about them muscling in and taking our business, it's proved to be entirely different. I think of Amethi as relatively earthy, and I know it still costs quite a lot for people to stay with us, or attend our courses, but it's not any different to what you might expect to pay elsewhere. And I like to think that we make it good value for money. The feedback from our guests backs this up.

The Harbour, however, is on another level when it comes to its pricing structure. But I think that the type of people who like to stay there feel reassured by this. They would not want to pay any less. Low-grade social media and TV 'personalities' often frequent the place. The women generally in snug white trousers and painfully pointy-heeled shoes, incredibly large sunglasses, and sweaters (never jumpers) resting neatly over their shoulders. Men in heavily shaded glasses, smart shirts, and creased trousers (I mean deliberately, sharply creased, not 'couldn't be arsed to get the iron out'), and shiny shoes. The Harbour Hotel crowd are generally easy to spot around town.

Our clientele, on the other hand, are more low-key, although I don't expect any of them are struggling for money. Often older couples, sometimes young professionals with money to spend on themselves, and sometimes full family groups, who take the whole place over. The cars which arrive tend to be good quality; not cheap by any means, but seldom flash. The Harbour Hotel's underground car park, which is guarded by sleek electric gates, is spacious and rarely full, allowing ample room for the fancy sports cars, Teslas and SUVs, which hare around the lanes behind the town.

I might sound disparaging, but actually I am just really pleased that Amethi and the Harbour Hotel are worlds apart. However, this didn't stop me popping in for a coffee one day, when I heard a certain actor was staying at the Harbour. "Lydia!" I'd whispered, seeing my previous employee, now the manager of the Harbour Hotel, about to whisk past me.

"Alice!" she'd smiled welcomingly. "How are you?" She eyed my stomach.

"Oh, you know. Getting bigger!" I stood to kiss her, noting her willowy frame. I still feel a degree of protective maternal instinct towards her. Remembering her studying so hard for her A-Levels while she was a waitress at the Sail Loft, back when I was the manager there. She was earnest and driven, and had no idea how beautiful she was. Now, she may have more of an idea, and she's as polished as any of her clientele, but nowhere near as flashy, and as genuine as ever. "How are you?"

"Tired!" she'd laughed.

"I know the feeling. Now, is he here?"

"He…? Oh…" she quickly cottoned on. "Well, you know I'm not allowed to give away any personal details of our guests," she said officiously, with a twinkle in her eye, whispering, "He is, but he's in his suite."

Of course. "Have you met him?"

"That would be telling."

"You have! You must have. What's he like?"

"He's very charming."

"I bet."

She looks both ways, to make sure nobody's listening, then leans towards me conspiratorially. I notice her cheeks are flushed. "Actually, he asked me out."

"What! No way. What did you say?"

"I said no. I have to, really. I can't be seen to be fraternising with our guests."

"They sound like Imogen's words."

"They are," she smiled ruefully. "But I suppose she's right. Anyway, why would I go out with a successful actor?"

"Yeah," I grinned. "Why would you want to do that? Oh, you actually mean that."

"They're all hot air and no substance. And he's probably got a girlfriend, if not more than one. So... no. Thank you, but no thank you."

"You are cool, Lydia. You are so cool!"

"I don't know about that," she smiled. "Look, I'd better get on. But it's so nice to see you, Alice."

"You too. It really is. Let's try and get together soon, shall we?"

"Yes, well I want you and Julie to come to our Christmas party here. But I would like to see you out of work. Somewhere a bit more relaxed." She was almost looking over her shoulder again. I suspect Imogen is a tough boss, but Lydia is more than up to it.

"Sure. You get going now, and I'll drop you a line to sort something out."

Of course, I haven't got round to doing that. Not because I don't want to, but because life is so hectic. I must sort something out before the baby comes along.

So I will go on Sunday, and poor old Sam will come along too, although I've told him he really doesn't have to. Karen and Ron have said they will look after Ben, who is invited to the Sail Loft party and will be shattered by the time Sunday night comes around. He won't be the only one.

Just two more weeks, I tell myself. *Then it's time to chill.*

9

Saturday morning brings a mist, although it is thin and hazy, betraying the blue sky and sun hiding just behind it. As I drive to Amethi, there are thicker patches, in the little dips in the roads, and the fields behind the hedgerows lie hidden beneath wispy layers.

I open the window, feeling a little of the mist drift into the car, and goose pimples run up my arms. I haven't seen another car yet, and if these roads and fields were not so familiar to me, I imagine this could be a little bit unnerving. But it's just ten minutes' drive from our house to Amethi, and I feel like I could do this drive with my eyes closed, although I won't be trying that any time soon.

As is often the case on changeover day, when I see all the existing guests' cars still parked up and locked, I experience a brief anxiety. They are meant to be out by ten, to allow time to prepare for the next influx. In reality, it is usually more like eleven. Julie and I ask Cindy to be here for half-ten, to allow a little leeway, so the guests don't feel harangued into leaving. I think it's good for Cindy, too. On Saturdays, I know she and Rod and their children like to have a sea-swim first thing, and breakfast on the beach. It's some rare family time, and I know it's precious.

I am early today, though. It's only about half past eight, and I expect the holiday lets are a hive of activity, with guests packing up, and hopefully finding time for one last coffee in the peace of this place before getting on the A30 and heading back home. I just want to get ahead of myself. I don't like to think I'm a control freak, but over time I

66

have definitely become more that way inclined. I just know that I feel more relaxed when I have a handle on things. Reluctantly, I had left Sam and Ben lying in bed, watching *Ben and Holly* on the tablet.

"Bye, Mummy," Ben had said absentmindedly, too enthralled in the programme to really notice me leaving.

"Bye, Ben. I'll be back for lunch, OK? Then we're going to a party at Nanny and Grandpa's later, OK?"

Normally, at the start of one of our yoga or writing weeks, I will stay on at Amethi to give our guests a proper welcome, but this is usually in the afternoon. Lizzie and Julie have insisted that they can handle it, and that I should go back home, and relax a bit before going to the Sail Loft.

"But I want to be here!" I'd moaned.

"Tough! You're going home to have a rest, so you can go to your mum and dad's later, and enjoy it," said Julie.

"I can do the welcome, Alice," said Lizzie. "And Julie, of course. Honestly, we've got it covered."

"OK," I'd said begrudgingly. I have to let go of the reins a bit, I know. So this morning I will meet Lizzie, to make sure she's happy with everything.

After I've pulled up, I open the door to let Meg out. She stays put. "Come on, Meg," I say. "Out you get!"

She's looking past me, intently, her ears pricked, and I turn to follow her gaze, but there's nothing there. The mist is still on the air, but it is thin here, and I have a clear view of the whole car park. "Come on, girl. I've got work to do." She stands slowly, and reluctantly, a low rumble of a growl in her throat. It puts the hairs on the back of my neck on end. I shake myself. Probably, she's seen a pheasant, or maybe even a fox. We get a lot of them up here. She wouldn't be happy to see either on her territory, and she does enjoy chasing those poor pheasants, sending them dizzyingly into the air in a panic, clucking and squawking, and beating their wings for all they're worth.

I take hold of her collar and gently pull, so she jumps reluctantly out. Closing the boot, I turn to walk towards the buildings, and after a moment Meg joins me, walking close to heel, not running off like she normally does.

Maybe the mist has spooked her. I'm glad it's lifting, and revealing the glorious blue of the sky. I know once the sun is up high, its rays will feel warm on my skin, even though we're deep into December. I can hardly believe that this time next week it will be Christmas Eve. One week, until I can relax. A bit. Then a few more days' work, and that's it for a while. Let's just forget the amount of work involved in looking after a baby, shall we? Pretend that I really will be having a break for a while.

Just as long as the baby doesn't make an early appearance, I will have a break of sorts. Maybe just a few hours a day, while Ben is at nursery and Karen's house, but still, I will have those precious hours all to myself. I cannot wait.

Meg's behaviour continues to be a little strange all morning. Something has put her on edge. She doesn't want to leave my side, and even comes up to the office with me. "Go on, Meg, go out," I say, but she refuses to go down the stairs, and I have to take hold of her collar again, and walk her with me. I take her outside, so she can have a run around while I work, but I find that once I'm in the fresh air I have a strong need to have a walk myself. I am struck by the birdsong, carrying across the fields from the woods. "Come on, let's find you a ball," I say, and Meg trots more willingly along now, sniffing the air, and even running off after a pair of wood pigeons.

The day is all but clear of mist now. I stop for a moment and breathe. Three slow inhalations – three longer breaths out. I feel good. I slept well last night, and I don't think I woke up once, until my alarm went off this morning. I've realised that perhaps I have not been feeling quite as well as I might have lately. Whether the high blood pressure has caused that, or being worn out has caused the high blood pressure, I am not sure. It's crept up on me, though, so it's just felt normal.

I place the palm of my right hand on my belly, trying to feel the shape of the baby. There is less room in there now for it to move around, and I occasionally see the outline of what might be an elbow, or a leg. I'm glad I'll be seeing Sandi again on Monday, and hope that there is good news about my blood pressure. I know I must listen to what everybody says, as annoying as it might be, and actually rest. For my own sake and the baby's.

We won't stay long at Mum and Dad's tonight, or at the Harbour party tomorrow. Sam will be pleased, and we'll at least have put in an appearance, so hopefully everybody will be happy.

Without warning, Meg goes dashing off into the woods, barking. "Meg!" I shout. "Leave it! Come back!" I hope it's not a rabbit she's spotted. She doesn't come back straight away, so I call her again and after a few moments, there is a rustling of leaves and she scoots towards me, not looking all that happy. Her tail is down, almost between her legs, and her ears are back. She's soon at my side, pushing her head against me.

"What is it, Meg? Did you get a telling off?" It shouldn't be a badger at this time of day, though I do sometimes fear she will have a run-in with one. I'm not convinced she'd emerge victorious from such an altercation. I peer between the trees, struck by the darkness in the woods. The floor is a carpet of decaying leaves, and although the branches are bare, they are strong against the sunlight today, which seems too weak to really break through. I couldn't see anything unless it moved. Like standing in the kitchen with the blinds open at night, I feel suddenly vulnerable. A target, if any were needed or wanted.

Nobody knows I'm here, I think, although that kind of thought never normally bothers me at Amethi. There was that time, when Tony was hounding us, and I knew somebody had been snooping at Amethi, that I was aware of my solitude and exposure out here. But I don't think I felt unsafe as such. And I don't now. Not really. But I am kind of rattled.

"Come on, look, here's the ball you lost the other day," I spot it in the hedgerow, and pick it up. Meg, instantly cheered, goes to grab it. "No, we'll take this back with us. You can have a good play with it while I'm in the office." I lift it out of her reach, and she doesn't jump up, but turns with me to follow the field-side path back towards the buildings. I'm happy to see windows and doors open in the holiday lets, and hear the sounds of activity carrying across the quiet of the morning. As I move closer, I feel easier. I love the woods, but there is something in the air today, or maybe Meg's weird behaviour is just putting me on edge.

As we come close to the edge of the field, I am startled by a noise from behind me. I think I even let out a little shriek. Meg turns and barks, and I turn, too. Something is swooping towards me, right towards my head, then it passes over, close enough that I'd felt the draught from its wide, strong wings. An owl!

I watch its progress, towards the buildings, over the roofs, and then it is gone. Bloody hell. It takes a while for my racing heart to calm down, and Meg is still agitated, too. She jumps at me, mouthing at my arm.

"Sit, Meg!" I say, sternly. She obeys, though doesn't look all that happy about it.

It was just an owl, and that must have been what got Meg's attention in the woods. I must say I'm relieved, and now excited by such a close encounter. What kind of owl was that, though? It looked like a barn owl, but I'm sure they're nocturnal.

"Must have been a short-eared owl," Sam tells me when I phone him from the Mowhay. I'm sitting waiting for Lizzie, and still exhilarated. I knew Sam would be interested. "They hunt during the day, and there's more of them around in winter, from places like Russia and Iceland. They're on the endangered list, though, so you were lucky to see one."

"I can't believe it was so close!"

"That must have been amazing. It was probably keeping an eye on a mouse or something, I bet you got in its way."

"Oops. Sorry, owl."

Meg had calmed quickly once I'd refilled her bowl of water, and given her the lost ball to play with. I can just see her, lying prone on the gravel, the ball not forgotten, just resting between her front paws. Hoping someone might come along and throw it for her.

I'm just relieved there was a simple, of this earth, explanation for her behaviour. I know it's silly, and I'm letting my imagination run away with me, but I was definitely a bit on edge.

10

I hear Lizzie's car, so I go into the kitchen and make us each a cup of tea, which I bring out into the sunshine. The day has kept its promise, and the sky is clear. I know Lizzie will prefer to sit outside while we can, and I am more than happy to.

Once she is settled, I tell her about my close encounter. "Wow!" she says, eyeing me closely. "You know what an owl symbolises, don't you, Alice?"

"No... what?"

"Wisdom. Deep inner knowledge. Supernatural power. It's also..." she trails off.

"What?" I ask again.

"Well, I don't strictly believe this, but some cultures consider it a bad omen. A foretelling of death." I tense a little, but I know it's just superstition. "It's also considered a symbol of change," she says more brightly.

"Well, that makes sense," I say. "Or, maybe... hear me out on this one... it was just out hunting."

"Yes, there is that!" Lizzie laughs. "I like your style, Alice. I always think you've got one foot in the spiritual camp, and one firmly grounded on Earth. It's a good way to be."

"Thank you, Lizzie." I feel pleased, somehow, that she's given me this much thought. It makes me want to tell her more. "You know, though, how last week you were telling me about that woman, who lost her baby?" I pretend to have forgotten Elizabeth's name, as though I haven't been partially obsessing about her.

"Yes?"

"Well, OK, this is going to sound weird, but I know I

can talk to you about these things."

"Without judgement," she says.

"Definitely, without judgement." Here goes. I look across the field as I talk, feeling a bit self-conscious. "Well, I think I had a dream about her the other night. Or she'd… she'd got into my dream, somehow. I know that sounds weird." I describe how I'd woken up, looking for Ben, and how disturbed my mind had been. And that other half-dream, where it had been me on the boat, holding onto my baby. "Actually, Lizzie, I'll come clean. I can't quite get her out of my mind. I even started looking for her, on Google. Trying to find her story."

"Ah," says Lizzie. "I don't think you'll find it online. Or if it's there, she won't be mentioned by name."

"Have you looked, too?"

"Kind of. Well, no. Not really."

"How do you know about her, then?" I imagine in Lizzie's circle these stories are passed around by word of mouth. Maybe there's some relation of Elizabeth's among Lizzie's friends.

"You'll never believe me."

"Try me."

"She told me."

"She…?"

"I said you wouldn't believe me."

It's true. My immediate reaction is disbelief. But I am intrigued. "Go on," I say.

"Well, I told you I hadn't encountered the smugglers, or whoever that boatload of men are, and it's true. But I did go down there one night, and I met her. Elizabeth. On the beach. I went looking for her, really. I was in a bad way. I haven't told you about this before, Alice, but I lost a baby, when I was a lot younger."

"Oh, Lizzie, I'm so sorry. I had no idea."

"No, well it's not something I talk about a lot. And I have been wondering whether or not to tell you, given your present state." Her green eyes are serious as she looks at me. I briefly think of Julie's and my initial reaction to Lizzie. A bit of a mad hippy, we both thought, if we're honest, but over the time I've known her, I've grown to love her, and respect her. She is generous and spirited, and kind and calm. I know Julie feels the same way. I had no idea Lizzie had such sadness in her past, but I suppose there is no reason I would have known.

"But I feel like it's the right thing to do. And I hope you'll forgive me if you disagree. I had a daughter, but she was stillborn. I gave birth to her at home, against the midwife's advice, and she was already dead." I feel tears spring to my eyes, as Lizzie continues. "I felt immense guilt, like I should have gone to hospital, but over time I've found assurance and some kind of peace, that the outcome would have been the same, wherever I'd given birth."

"I am so sorry," I say again.

"So, anyway, back then, I heard the story, about the woman who'd lost her baby to the sea, and how she wanders the beach at night. I went out looking for her. I wanted to join her in grief. I half-wanted the sea to swallow me up, I think, but I knew that wasn't really the right thing. Still, I went down there one night."

"Alone?" I ask, imagining picking my way through those woods to the cove, in the dead of night. I don't think I could do it. But Lizzie is braver than me.

"Alone," she confirms. "And I sat on the steps, and watched and waited. And cried. I cried a lot. Then I felt her. Next to me. I didn't see her, but I knew she was there."

My arms and neck prickle.

"It wasn't scary, Alice," Lizzie says. "It was comforting. I felt her, and I knew her, and I knew her name. And her baby's name. I had called my girl Anise, and she'd been taken away to the hospital, and I wish that she hadn't. I never saw her again. I wish that I'd kept her, and buried her. But it wasn't the way then. There was very little choice. I should have been stronger," she says with feeling.

"Don't say that, Lizzie. How on earth can you be strong in that situation?" I am crying now, and she looks at me, aghast.

"Oh my god, Alice, how can I be telling you this, when you're so close to giving birth? I am so sorry. I didn't want to upset you, and I don't want to worry you. This isn't how it's going to be for you, you know."

She can't possibly know that, but I understand. "Lizzie," I say. "I know that because this awful thing happened to you, it doesn't mean it's going to happen to me, too. I realise that these things happen, and you sharing your story hasn't made me worried – no more than I already was, anyway. I am so glad you told me. Honestly, I feel honoured that you'd want to."

I put my hand on hers, and she smiles at me. My attention is caught by a butterfly dancing through the air behind her. I hope it finds somewhere warm and safe for the rest of winter, just in case we don't get to keep this beautiful weather.

"It won't be like that for you, Alice. And this all began with the owl, didn't it? There was an owl that night, in the woods, when I went down to the beach. I remember hearing it above me, while I walked down there. It was like it was never far away, following me, from the treetops. It was a warm, clear night, and I ended up sleeping on the beach, beneath the stars. I felt as though that owl, and

Elizabeth, were keeping watch on me. And in the morning, the sadness wasn't gone – it never has – but I did feel clearer-headed. Like I knew it wasn't my fault, what had happened to Anise. And that even though I wish I'd kept her with me – kept her body, I mean – it was OK. She was OK. I've tried to hold on to that feeling, and it hasn't always been easy. But I always talk to her, and I'm always looking for her. It's what has led me to where I am, trying to find some meaning, and some kind of... evidence... that this isn't all there is. Because I couldn't bear it if it was, Alice, and if I'm never to see my girl again."

She is crying again, but I hold my own tears back now. This is Lizzie's sorrow, not mine. "Oh, Lizzie," I murmur.

"Yes, well," she seems to shake herself a little. "Now you know. Thank you for listening."

"Any time," I say. "Honestly, any time." But I feel like she has maybe been through this as many times as she needs to, and has a handle on it, so that she doesn't need support from me, or to keep dragging it all up again. "I am so glad you told me, Lizzie. Really."

"Well, you're a good'un, Alice. And you know what else owls represent? Free-thinkers. Oddballs." I laugh. "You're a bit of an oddball, Alice, even if it's not immediately apparent. And I mean that as a compliment. Owls see what others don't, and I think you're like that."

I don't know what to say.

"I mean it. You hold on to your ideas, and your visions, and your dreams, and don't let people put you off."

I can feel myself blushing.

"And you don't like the spotlight on you, do you? I get that. So, enough of the compliments! Let's get this week sorted so you can get home to your little boy."

"Let's," I say. Part of me doesn't want to leave this

conversation here. I am full of emotion at what happened to Lizzie and her little girl, but she won't thank me for overdoing the sympathy, and I understand that. "I hope you have a fantastic week," I say instead.

"Thank you, Alice." She smiles, and I hope that I have somehow conveyed everything that I want to.

11

"It looks so beautiful!" I am standing in the hallway of the Sail Loft with Mum, gazing at the silvery Christmas tree. Ben, hopeful of a cup of apple juice, has already run off in the direction of the bar with Dad, followed by Sam, hopeful of a bottle of beer. There is much noise from the bar, and the dining room, and I know I will have to go and be sociable in a moment or two. But I just want to appreciate this place, for a few moments. This beautiful old merchant's house, now a hotel (never a B&B, according to Bea, who used to run it. Maybe just because that would be too many Bs) – which has been such an important part of my life in Cornwall. Entrusted with managing the place by Bea when she went off to America, it's hard to explain quite how much the Sail Loft means to me. Now it's Mum and Dad's, and, after a bit of a rocky start, they seem to love it, maybe as much as I do.

Mum has wrapped garlands around the banisters, and the wood-panelled walls are adorned with strings of cards from family, friends, and even past guests who have also formed an attachment to the place. I always think houses have their own very particular feel and smell, and the Sail Loft certainly has. I remember being struck by it when I walked back through the door, into Bea's arms, when I came to work here that second time. It transported me back ten years. Now, while it has retained that familiar scent and atmosphere, it has also taken on a little of those qualities that I associate with Mum and Dad, and our old house – my childhood home – which they sold some time

78

ago. Today, there is also the smell of buffet food, and mulled wine. It's very warm, and very welcoming.

"I'd better go and be the genial host," Mum smiles. "Are you coming?"

I hesitate and, as Mum always does, she gets it. "Do you want a few minutes? Go on through to the office if you want to. You can come and join us in a bit. The mulled wine and prosecco are flowing, and I think half the guests are a bit sozzled already. In the nicest possible way, I don't think anyone will miss you."

"No offence, eh!" I laugh. "Will you just let Sam know where I am?"

"Of course."

I wander gratefully into the office, closing the heavy door behind me. Here is the same furniture there has always been. Bea inherited it from the owners previous to her, and I have no idea where they got it from, but it feels like it might always have been here. The clock ticks gently away on the mantelpiece, and I sit in the large leather-covered chair, folding my hands across my belly.

When I was working here alone, I would often imagine that there were ghosts in and around the Sail Loft. Spirits of previous residents, keeping an eye on the old place. It's funny, that. I have always half-believed in these things – that the life we know does not have to be all the life there is. And I love ghost stories, and horror films, but I have never really felt like I have encountered anything of the sort in real life, or been scared that I might.

It seems strange, then, that Lizzie's story about Elizabeth Grayley has hooked me for some reason - but then again, I am very tired, and very pregnant. I am also flooded with hormones and nerves and worries, about the baby, and the birth, and Ben. Perhaps this is all manifesting in some weird kind of fixation about what happened to Elizabeth. If indeed there really was an Elizabeth, I remind myself, trying to hang on to a healthy level of scepticism.

I close my eyes, and breathe in deeply. *Are you there?* I ask the spirits of the Sail Loft, internally, before kicking myself for being an idiot. What am I playing at? And if there are such things as ghosts, do I really think they can read my mind? But Lizzie said she communicated with Elizabeth through thought. But then again, that's Lizzie.

I hear a gentle knock on the door, and Sam pushes it open. I am grateful to see my sensible, grounded, husband's face. I can't help but smile at him. He was a beautiful, golden boy when I met him, and he's now a man – broader, with slightly less hair, and slightly bigger muscles (and more stubble). Possibly slightly more belly, too, but we will gloss over that. Who I am I to talk, anyway?

"You OK?" he whispers.

"Yes!" I whisper as loudly as I can, grinning at him. "We can talk, you know. I'm not hiding. Well, not really…"

"You can't make me be the sociable one," he grins back. "That is not how our relationship works. You're the one with the talk."

"What? I don't know what you mean!"

"I'm the strong, silent type, remember?"

"Hmm. I suppose I should show my face," I acknowledge. "Is Ben behaving himself?"

"He's loving it. Now he really is the life and soul of the party. Entertaining all the grown-ups. Your dad's loving showing him off."

"I bet!" I feel that familiar rush of love for my little boy, and happiness at my situation. I am too lucky, I know it, and I don't know what I've done to deserve it.

I stand, with a little bit of effort, and Sam steps forward, takes my hands, and kisses me. "Reminiscing?" he asks.

"A little."

"The good old days. When you were young, free and single?"

"They were good days – but these are better." I kiss him back, then kiss him a little more.

"We never did do it in here, did we?" Sam asks. "I always wanted to… you know, get you on this big old desk…"

"It would collapse under my weight now," I say, happy that Sam still feels like this about me, and also that I feel a bit turned on by it all. I had wondered if I'd ever feel like that again. Hopefully, one day, once I'm over the birth… maybe I'll feel like my body is mine again.

"I don't think so," he says, moving behind me, his arms around my waist, on my belly, in my top…

"Sam!" I say, pretend-shocked. "This is the Sail Loft Soiree. It is not *that* kind of party, I'll have you know."

"It should be. Isn't there a key to that door?"

"You know there is. But you know we can't."

"Not fair…" he groans.

"That's life, I'm afraid." I smile and kiss him again, teasingly. "Now come on, there is schmoozing to be done!"

"Schmoozing, my arse," I hear him mutter behind me as I turn and head towards the door.

"What was that?"

"Nothing, darling."

I grin and I open the door, ushering him through into the warmth and the general hubbub of the party.

Ben, as Sam had said, is loving the attention he's getting. He is currently talking to Linda, one of the women from the bakery that supplies the Sail Loft.

"There you are!" he says to me, like he's the grown-up.

It makes Linda laugh.

"Here I am," I confirm, smiling. "How are you, Linda? Looking forward to Christmas?"

"I can't wait, I'm shattered!" she says. "And I've just been hearing from Ben all about how he's going to be a big brother soon."

"As if that wasn't obvious already," I say ruefully, eyeing my protruding belly.

"Well, you look lovely, Alice, and your eyes are twinkling."

Probably thanks to Sam in the office. "Thank you, Linda. I've been feeling fairly worn out, but I'm on the home strait now. We've got the yoga retreat this week, then Christmas, then New Year." I count them off on my fingers. This little list is becoming a bit of a mantra. And soon I'll be able to tick off the yoga. But I don't want to rush anything. *Don't wish your life away,* Mum used to say to me when I was little, and looking forward to a party, or a birthday, or Christmas. These words meant very little to me back then, but now I get it.

It's like when everyone tells you that time will fly with your children. One minute they're a tiny helpless baby, the next they're packed and off to Uni, or a job, or travelling, never to return. There is still plenty of time for us, but already Ben is on his way to being three. In another year and a half, he'll be starting school. And yet, our new little one has barely begun. There is plenty of time yet. But I do not want to take anything for granted. Not until this baby is in my arms. And even then, I know, those first few weeks will be tinged with anxiety. I felt that with Ben, until he was a little older and stronger. When they are first born and utterly helpless, it is such a huge weight of responsibility, and there are so many unknowns. Of course,

82

this is still the case as they grow and our responsibility doesn't lessen. We've had it drilled into us, that we should recognise the symptoms of meningitis, or sepsis, or diabetes, or a thousand other illnesses. If we miss something, we risk everything.

I think of Lizzie, and that other Elizabeth, too. Their babies, Anise and Rose. I can't bear it, and I know that although pregnancy, and childbirth, and motherhood, are such everyday things, they also have the potential for danger, and loss, and unbearable sadness. But it's also a time of peace and excitement, and huge emotions that I could never have imagined. I just have to stay calm and sensible, and remind myself I have no need to worry. Worrying is not going to help my blood pressure.

All of this is flying through my head while Linda tells me to look after myself. I promise her I will. And then Mum is at my side, with Janet from the Bluebell Hotel.

Janet kisses me. "You're looking well, Alice," she says, and I smile. If I look well, I probably am well, I think. "And I hear you're going to the swanky Harbour Hotel do tomorrow," she raises her eyebrows. "Us mere mortals haven't been invited, of course."

"Oh well, it's just because of Julie and me knowing Lydia, really. But I must admit, I'm intrigued," I grin.

"And is you-know-who going to be there?"

"Who?"

"You know! Him! The actor. Si whatshisname."

"Si Davey?" It's news to me if he is.

"Yes, I heard it from Christine, whose daughter's friend waitresses there. They're all of a twitter about it!"

My mind flicks to Lydia. I wonder if she invited him. If she's not actually as cool towards him as she'd suggested. But it's more likely down to Imogen. She'll have overseen the whole guest list. I wonder how Lydia got me and Julie on it. "I bet they are," I smile. "Well, I'll see if I can get a selfie with him, shall I?"

"Oh yes, do!" Janet says.

"I'll do my best!"

It's not long before I begin to feel tired, and I can tell Ben is much the same. He's lost his chattiness now and is sitting on the seat behind me, his eyes slightly glazed. I know I only have to say the word to Sam and he'll have our coats, bags and car keys in his hand, quick as a flash. I catch his eye from across the room. He is cornered by Eric, a lovely guy from the Christmas Lights committee, who is always trying to get Sam to join the open water swimming club that he runs.

Sam's eyes light up. I see him put his hand on Eric's arm, apologetically, and they both look over towards me. I smile at Eric contritely. Sam starts to make his way through the crowd, getting Dad's attention to tell him we're leaving. Mum is nearby, and I reach out to her to let her know. "We're off, Mum. I'll call you tomorrow. Enjoy the rest of the evening."

"I will," she says, then steps closer. "But I don't want this to go on too long. We've got guests to get up and cook for tomorrow. Mind you, I'm not sure Mr and Mrs Parker are going to feel too much like an early morning!" She gestures to a couple who are sitting at the bar, both bent double with laughter about something.

"I see what you mean," I say.

"But I still want this lot gone by eleven!"

"Good luck, Mum. I suppose you can tell them they have to, for the sake of your other, more sober, guests."

"I'll have to."

"They're just having too much fun, Mum. Take it as a compliment."

"I suppose," she says, dubiously.

"Definitely." I kiss her as Sam reaches my side, swinging Ben up and into the air.

"Bye, Sue," says Sam, also kissing her, and moving Ben forward so he can do the same. His little arms reach around my mum's neck.

"Bye, Sam. And bye, little Ben. You have a good night's sleep, and let your mum and dad have a lie-in tomorrow, OK? Oh, and Alice... don't forget that selfie!"

At the top of the Sail Loft steps, I breathe in deeply. It is a relief to be out in the open, and just drink in the sight of the town laid out before us. Christmas trees and lights adorn the streets, the church star sitting loftily above them all.

"Shall we do a little drive around town?" Sam asks, Ben clinging tightly to him. "Take a look at all the lights? What do you think, Ben?"

"Yes please, Daddy," says Ben, sleepily. I have a feeling he won't stay awake long, but I love the idea.

"That sounds really nice," I say, and I put my hand in Sam's free one. We walk to the car, and Sam fastens Ben into his seat, while I try to squeeze into mine. I need to put it back even further. I let out a groan.

"Are you OK?" Sam asks, his face pure concern.

"I'm fine!" I laugh. "Just trying to get into the car, that's all."

"Are you sure?"

"I am, perfectly. I promise I'd let you know if it was anything else."

It takes a bit of work to turn in my seat, but I see Ben

secured in his, looking very content. He smiles at me, and my heart melts. "OK back there?"

He nods happily.

"Do you want Tiger?"

"Yes please, Mummy."

I pass the toy back to Ben and, as predicted, he is fast asleep almost as soon as Sam has started the engine.

"Shall we get him back home?" Sam asks.

"Yes, but let's have a little detour, shall we? I want to see the town at night!"

"Alright, then. Let's start with the old place."

Sam pulls onto the steep street where my old house is. I say 'my old house', but it was never really mine – not in any legal ownership kind of way. But as I've lived there multiple times now, with Julie and David, then just Julie, then with Sam, Ben and Sophie, it feels very much like I have a stake in it. Now it belongs to a pair of artists and Sam slows the car as we pass by, admiring the window scene they've created. It's like a silhouette of the town houses and rooftops, with lights shining behind cut-out windows. The church tower is the highest point, and they've put a replica of the star at the very top.

"I might have known they'd do something bloody great," I say.

"Do you miss living there?"

"Yes and no. Maybe there's a small part of me that hopes we'll find a way back there one day! But that's not very likely."

"You never know," says Sam. "But also, we've moved on. Onwards and upwards, Griffiths!" he grins.

"Onwards and upwards," I agree. He drives on, and we are soon passing the end of Fore Street, and turning past the lifeboat station onto the harbour road. All the restaurants and shops are lit with different colours, while the lifeboat station has a projector shining onto its front, casting changing colours and images of the boat, and the crew, and all the other volunteers, onto the huge glass doors. It makes me catch my breath, and I think it would anyway, thinking of what those people do, and the situations they put themselves in, all year round, but all the more so as I remember that terrifying night earlier this year, when Sam was one of those people lucky enough to be rescued.

Sam is quiet, too, and pulls the car over at the far end of the road, where we stop and just watch for a while, in silence.

"What a year," he says finally.

"Yep." I put my hand on his arm. There are so many things I could say – how glad I am that he is here, and OK, and that they found him, and rescued him. But he knows all that already. It does not need to be said. "I wonder what next year will be bring."

"Hopefully some peace and quiet."

"You do know we're about to have another baby?"

"Yes, well I expect it to be very peaceful and quiet."

"It's bound to be."

The harbour pier is adorned with coloured lights, and the lighthouse wrapped in them, in a spiral reminiscent of a helter-skelter. Bobbing on the waves below the wall is a small boat, which I happen to know belongs to Eric (he of the Christmas light committee and swim club), displaying the words 'Merry Christmas' one moment, followed by 'Nadelik Lowen' (the Cornish language version) the next.

"We're so lucky to live here," I say.

"Not bored yet, then?"

"Never!"

"Shall we?" Sam gestures to the road.

"Drive on!"

Through the network of narrow streets we go, and around the car park at the bottom of the Island. The chapel is lit up against the darkness, and I would love to go up there now – hear the sea, and feel the wind against my skin in the darkness. Look back at the lights of the town. To get there, however, would mean huffing and puffing up the steep slope, and then having to sit and catch my breath for a good five minutes. Besides which, Ben is asleep in the back of the car, and we need to get him home.

Next year, I tell myself.

We exit the car park and drive along towards the surfing beach, then up and around the back of town, until we reach home. The house is in darkness, but Sam bounds in, switching on the lights in the hallway light and the landing. "I'll come back for Ben," he whispers, before he goes, and he is good to his word, lifting our little son as carefully as possible, so as not to disturb him. Of course, he's going to have to get him ready for bed once we're in the house anyway, but it's a challenge between us, to see if we can ever transfer Ben from the car to his bed and keep him asleep.

I stop for a moment, looking along the street. Many of the curtains are drawn, but glowing softly with lights from inside, while a couple of doors along, the window displays a huge tree, its branches pressed up against the glass, twinkling with lights, and, as I know from walking past in the daytime, scattered liberally with baubles and candy canes, and foil-wrapped chocolates.

It makes me smile, and I check the sky to see if it's a clear night, but clouds are moving rapidly across it, obscuring and then occasionally revealing the moon.

Across the road, there is a loud rustling in the hedge. The sound startles me, as I am suddenly aware that Sam and Ben are inside, upstairs, and there is nobody here on the street except me. It will just be an animal, of course, but even so, it makes me hurry indoors.

I can hear Sam talking upstairs, perhaps reading Ben a story. Meg is crying behind the kitchen door, waiting to be let out. I open the door and she bounces through, as overjoyed to see me as if I have been gone for weeks, not hours. Then she stops, her ears pricked, and rushes to the door, her barks resounding in the hallway.

"Shush, Meg. There's nobody there. Shhh." I sit on the stairs and she comes to me, letting me hold her close, but still straining slightly towards the door. She emits a slight growl, and another bark. "There's nobody there," I say again, but it's put me on edge. "Come on, let's put the kettle on." Meg follows me into the kitchen, and lies on the floor, but she's not quite relaxed. Not quite happy. I put the radio on, and realise I'm shaking a little.

This is silly, I tell myself. Maybe that was a fox or something in the hedge, and that's what's set Meg off. *There is always a rational explanation.* Those were Sam's words, and I'm sure he's right. Nevertheless, I'm happier when he comes downstairs, knowing Ben is now safely asleep in his own bed, and Sam is by my side.

Predictably, Meg doesn't make a peep for the rest of the evening. Sam asks why she was barking, and I tell him it was a cat outside. After we've watched a bit of TV and decided it's time for sleep, our dog trots obediently out for a wee, then settles into her bed for the night.

Which should, of course, reassure me, but it takes me some time to get to sleep and, once Sam is breathing deeply, I get up and peek through the curtains to the street outside. The cloud cover has gone now, revealing the moon in its fullness. With the aid of the streetlights, it illuminates the pavement, and I can see that all is quiet and still. I hear an owl hoot and the sound comforts me.

Closing the curtains, I tiptoe through to check on Ben. He is fine, his stars lighting his room, and his duvet on the floor, as always. I pick it back up and tuck him in, and I can't help leaving our door open, just a little, so I can keep half an ear open through the night. Back in bed, the baby kicking away merrily, I am shattered but wide awake. I just can't shake the thought that it wasn't an animal in the bushes. That it was somebody, or something, watching me. But why make a noise? It was almost as if it wanted to draw attention to itself.

You're being ridiculous, Alice, I tell myself firmly. *Irrational. Hormonal.* I try to think instead of a summer day. A walk along the town beaches and up onto the headland. Hot sun beating down. Sea gentle, glossy and calm. I imagine floating on the placid waves, the sun just behind me and the sky above a clear, sapphire blue. My hair spreading out around my shoulders and tiny beads of saltwater speckling my skin.

Slowly, slowly, I start to feel as though the sun really is on my skin, and I allow myself to sink into the safety of sleep.

12

"I've definitely been having more strange dreams," I say to Sandi, feeling the need to confess my recent anxieties to somebody – to seek some reassurance.

"What do you mean by strange?" she laughs. "Are we talking sexy stuff?"

"No!" I laugh. "Although I did see Si Davey at the Harbour Hotel party last night."

"Well, any thoughts or feelings relating to Si Davey would be perfectly normal, and not just during pregnancy!"

"But no, it wasn't anything like that. It's... oh, it's just daft. I think I've been having weird dreams, and they're getting into my head."

"Ah well, that does sound pretty normal to me. I think I said before, they believe it's to do with hormone production. Isn't everything, when you're pregnant? Anyway, you might have more vivid dreams, and it can be easier to recall them, too."

I don't want to admit to her that it's not just dreams that are bothering me. That I haven't quite been able to shake that sense of fear I felt on Saturday night. It's almost as if saying it out loud will make it more real. Or have her packing me off to hospital.

As she puts the blood pressure cuff around my arm, she says, "Don't tense up. Try and take a couple of slow breaths, and then we'll do it. You'll be worrying about it being higher, I know."

"I am, a bit."

"There we go. Right... it will start to feel a bit tight. I

don't know why I'm telling you that, you know the drill. So, what are these dreams about?"

"It sounds a bit stupid, but like I'm being watched."

"Watched?" she raises an eyebrow. "By a man? A monster? A ghost? Keep still," she reminds me. "That's it."

"I think it is… a ghost," I say, watching her face for her reaction.

"Oh yeah? Like a Scooby Doo kind of thing?"

"No, like… oh, I know I am going to sound completely mad now."

"No, go on." She jots down the numbers from the monitor, turning it to show me. "Look, it's pretty much the same. Still a little on the high side, but it's not any worse, which is encouraging."

I am relieved by that at least. And as she seems to be a willing audience, I explain to her about going to the beach with Lizzie, and about Elizabeth, and Rose, and how I can't seem to quite shake them from my head.

She's a good listener, Sandi. "Sounds to me like you're projecting your fears about this pregnancy and this baby, and maybe even the birth, my love. It's perfectly normal."

"Is it?"

"Yes, yes, dreams are the perfect manifestation of anxiety. You're dreaming about this… Elizabeth?" she checks, and I nod. "And she's a young woman – a young mother, like you. And she suffered something like your worst fear – the death of a child." I nod again. "I'd say it's perfectly natural that you've put yourself in this woman's place, and this has seeped into your subconscious. Honestly, Alice, you've nothing to worry about. You're not losing it, I promise. I've heard far worse, believe me! The best thing you can do is try to relax."

Put like this, it all starts to sound very rational and

sensible. *There is always a rational explanation.* The only thing is, of course, I haven't told Sandi that I've been experiencing things in the real world, not just my dreams. And there's Meg's strange behaviour, too. But then, if I'm on edge, I might be causing Meg to feel anxious, too.

The best thing I can do is try to unwind a little. Take things easy. How many times do people have to tell me this before I take their advice?

We are edging towards Christmas, with less than a week to go. I plan to make it to the solstice celebration, which is a very early start, but aside from that, I am under strict instructions from Lizzie and Julie that I must stay at home, and check emails if I must, but nothing more strenuous than that. My blood pressure is not any worse than it was, and Sandi doesn't seem too concerned, so I think it's time to try and lay off all this worrying, and instead concentrate on all the things I've got to look forward to.

"Anyway," says Sandi, "enough about ghosts. Tell me all about Mr Davey and this party, please!"

❅ ❆ ❅

I had driven into town, picking Julie and Luke up. Sam and Luke both looked very handsome in tuxedos, though Sam kept fidgeting with his bow tie, and pulling at his collar. "I hate this shit," he grumbled.

"Think of the delicious food and free-flowing beer, and you might be able to cope with it," I said.

"I'd rather just be at home with the TV on, and a bag of crisps."

"I know, I know, and you know I'm the same, really."

"Rubbish! You want to see that actor bloke."

"Si Davey!" Julie called from the back. "Don't pretend

you can't remember his name! It's OK to have a man crush, you know, Sam."

"I'll have you know I'm very modern and with-it," he retorted.

"Just using the term 'with-it' kind of suggests otherwise," Julie laughed, and I joined in.

"Don't know what you're laughing at, Griffiths. You married me!"

"Out of sympathy," I said.

"Oh yeah?"

I cast a sidelong glance at Sam and for a moment my stomach flipped, like it used to, when we were young and childless, and lived for the moment. Or it could have been the baby. Or indigestion.

"Get a room, you two," said Julie.

Rather than get stuck in the underground car park, we left the car at the station. I was grateful that being pregnant gave me the perfect excuse to wear flat shoes, especially on the steep stone steps from the car park. Julie, of course, managed them with no problem, looking elegant and effortlessly gorgeous, in a jade-green shift dress and heels which I couldn't walk in even if I wasn't pregnant. Predictably, heads turned towards her as we entered the hotel and were greeted by a smartly dressed young man who took our coats, and by Lydia, who was looking equally as beautiful as Julie, in a floor-length black dress with a halter-neck. She must have been wearing heels as well and I stood between her and my friend, feeling every inch the frumpy short-arse.

"You look gorgeous," Sam whispered in my ear, with perfect timing. "Maybe we *should* get a room!"

"If we want to bankrupt ourselves," I whispered back,

but felt pleased. I pushed back my shoulders, and felt my chin lift slightly. *Be proud, Griffiths*, I thought, then corrected myself: *Branvall*. That was enough to give me the lift I needed.

Lydia ushered us along. "I'll come and chat properly later," she said apologetically.

We walked into the main dining room, which was glittering with lights, and whitened teeth. In the window, a stupendous tree stood, as elegant as Lydia, twinkling and glistening above an array of expensive-looking gift bags.

"Do you think we get one of those?" I murmured to Julie.

"I hope so!" she said. "We are guests, after all."

"But maybe… lower tier guests?" I laughed.

"Don't you believe it, Alice. We're every inch as good as… oh my god, is that Si Davey?"

I followed Julie's line of sight, towards the bar. There was Imogen, flanked by a tall older gentleman, and seemingly hemming the actor in, so that he couldn't get away even if he wanted to. I watched as Imogen threw back her head and laughed at something Si had said.

"He asked Lydia out," I said.

"He what?" Julie screeched, making a number of heads turn.

"I forgot to tell you."

"How on earth could you forget to tell me that, Alice?"

"She said no."

"She what?" This at a slightly lower level. Luke, who had been chatting with Sam, looked at her curiously.

"Lydia was only asked out by this generation's hottest actor!" Julie hissed at him, while I looked around, hoping nobody was listening. "And she said no!"

Luke looked as interested in this as I'd expect. Not very.

"Men," Julie tutted. "I wonder if he's brought somebody

with him tonight. Make Lydia jealous."

"He's probably forgotten all about her by now," I said. "He must have women throwing themselves at him all the time."

"I guess. Still… bet she wishes she'd said yes now."

There was a slight screech of feedback, and we looked around to see Imogen standing on a dais by the Christmas tree. "Ladies and gentlemen, thank you all so much for coming to see us in the little old town by the sea." Julie nudged me. "It's been a dream of mine, since I was a little girl, to run a hotel here. I used to come here and visit my grandmother, and I fell in love with the place. I am very grateful to have been welcomed with open arms by the local community–" This was news to me, I've heard she has turned down all invites to the networking club, and requests for donations to the Christmas lights fund, saying she preferred to do things her own way - "and I feel quite the local myself now. I am so proud of what we have achieved at the Harbour Hotel, and I owe no small thanks to my wonderful manager, Lydia. Lyd, will you come up here?" I saw a few people moving out of the way, as Lydia made her way to the stage, looking more than a little bit shy, and all the more beautiful for it. I wondered if Si was watching, and cast a glance around the room, but I couldn't see him anywhere.

"I'd like to say a huge thank you to you, Lydia, and I bought you a little something to wish you a merry Christmas." Imogen presented Lydia with a small gift bag. "Open it," she insisted, with something of a forced smile.

"Now? It's not Christmas yet," Lydia said, to a smattering of laughter.

"Yes, now, you silly girl!" Imogen said, and I felt my hackles rise. Lydia didn't look too pleased, either.

"Some way to thank her," Julie muttered.

Lydia did as she was told, and removed a sleek box from the bag. Opening the box, she looked very surprised.

"That's right, a Thomas Sabo," Imogen turned, announcing this to the crowd as much as Lydia. "I hope you like it, Lydia. And should help your time-keeping too," she said with a little light laugh, which I noted was reciprocated slightly awkwardly by just a handful of people.

Lydia looked gobsmacked, but remained composed. "Thank you, Imogen. I'm afraid I haven't got you anything." And she left the stage.

Imogen was flustered for just a moment, then regained her composure. "My wonderful manager, everybody," she said, leading the applause, but the look on her face didn't match her words.

"I'm going to find Lydia," I said to Sam, squeezing his hand and trying to make my way through the room without knocking anyone's drink. I tried to keep an eye on Lydia's progress, and saw her exit the room, and head down the stairs to the ladies' toilets. I followed her, into the softly-lit, plush room. All the cubicles were empty but for one.

"Lydia?" I asked.

"Alice?" The door was unlocked, and Lydia came through it. She looked unhappy.

"Are you alright?" I asked. "That was... that seemed a bit out of order, of Imogen, I mean."

"She's a bitch," she said matter-of-factly. "That won't surprise you, Alice. You can see through her."

"But I thought you liked it here?"

"Oh, I do! It's a dream job, in so many ways. I love the hotel, and the business side of things, and when she's not here it's fantastic. That's why I stay. Plus, she doesn't scare me. She's just a tired old..."

The door swung open and Imogen swanned in. "Don't stop there, Lydia, please. It sounds like you were just getting started."

"I…" Lydia looked shocked.

"Don't worry, darling, you're right. I am a bitch. How do you think I got to where I am today? Oh, hello, Alex," she said to me, as though she'd only just noticed me, and I'm sure she knows my name really. She was slurring her words slightly, and had clearly had a drink or two – or a drink or two too many.

"Imogen." I nodded.

"Didn't she used to work for you? I imagine you were a much nicer boss than me. You just can't quite offer the same opportunities, though, can you?"

"*I* wouldn't be where *I* am today, without Alice," Lydia said. "And neither of us has felt the need to be a bitch to achieve things."

"Well," Imogen was touching up her lipstick, "that's why I own this place, and you only manage it. And Alice has that – rustic, shall we say? – heap of old buildings out of town."

I looked at Lydia, and she raised her eyebrows. "Imogen, we don't have to stay and listen to this."

"No, you don't. Off you go, then. Enjoy the party."

We left the toilets. I was fuming. "Are you really going to let her talk to you like that?"

"It's perfectly normal, honestly, Alice. She probably won't even remember tomorrow. She's got a bit of a drinking problem."

"But that's no excuse."

"No, but, like I say, she's only a pain when she's here. When she's not, I can do things my way. And I do love it," she said, her eyes shining.

98

"I can see that. Well, as long as you can handle her."

"I can."

"Lydia?" At the top of the stairs was none other than Si Davey. I immediately felt like a giggly schoolgirl, but Lydia was fantastically composed, and professional.

"Oh, hello. How are you? I hope you're enjoying the party."

"It's… interesting. Listen," his eyes strayed to me, and I flashed him an awkward smile. "I was hoping I'd see you. I was hoping… you might have changed your mind."

Lydia turned to me. "I'd better go and find Sam," I said, hoping I was being subtle enough. "I'll see you in a bit, Lydia. Nice to, erm, meet you, erm…"

"Simon," he put out his hand. As if he could possibly think I didn't know his name.

I took his hand faintly.

"See you in a bit, Alice," Lydia said, smiling.

"Yes, of course. See you in a bit."

Si Davey is very tall, and between him and Lydia, I felt like I could be her mum. Or her chaperone, like beautiful young women used to have when they were travelling around Europe, before they were married off to suitable young men.

I walked away with my head held as high as possible, and then once I was through the door to the dining room, I rushed to find Julie, Luke and Sam.

"I just… I just shook hands with Si Davey!" I exclaimed as quietly as I could.

"No way!" shrieked Julie, while Sam and Luke looked nonplussed.

"Yes, I… I think he's about to ask Lydia out again."

"What! No way!" I became aware that Julie had perhaps had a drink too many.

"Yes. I had to leave them to it. He was very nice and charming…"

"Do I have to worry about this?" Sam said.

"No! No, because he's asking Lydia out, and anyway, he's far too young for me, but he's perfect for Lydia, and I felt like her mum. He'd make a lovely son-in-law."

"Lydia is only ten years younger than you, Alice," Julie reminded me.

"I know, but I feel so old, and so… matronly, next to her. And next to him. Next to Si Davey. Si Davey!"

"Bloody hell, Alice, calm down or you'll be giving birth in here," Luke said drily.

"You're right. But how exciting. But Imogen… oh my god." I told them about the scene in the toilet.

"Silly old bitch," said Luke.

"Exactly."

"Sounds like Lydia can handle herself, though," said Julie. "Good on her. And now she's about to bag a gorgeous actor."

❄ ❄ ❄

We were indeed given a gift bag each before we left, though I wondered if there were two tiers of gift bags as well as guests. We had some of the toiletries which I am pretty sure are used in the Harbour Hotel bathrooms – nice, and pricey, but still… and some chocolates.

"Is that it?" Julie asked, disappointed. "I'm surprised the shampoo's not already been opened!"

"A gift bag's a gift bag, Julie," said Luke. "Me and Sam didn't get nothing."

"Oh, so you *did* get *something*?" Julie loves correcting Luke's English.

"Alright, smartarse," he said, drawing her in for a kiss.

"Get a room, you two," I echoed Julie's line from earlier.

We dropped them off and by the time we were home, I was shattered. Sam opened the door and let me in first, before I'd had the chance to contemplate whether or not there was a presence hiding in the bushes.

Karen came into the hallway, smiling. "He's been good as gold," she said. "Did you two have a good time?"

"We did, thanks."

"Well, I bet you're all partied out, aren't you? We'll leave you to it. Ron!" she called, as quietly as she could.

He came into the hallway, putting his arm around Karen, and kissing her on the cheek. They looked really loved up, and I'm so genuinely happy for Karen that she came back to Cornwall. I am pleased for Sam, too, despite his protestations about what a nuisance she is. I know he's glad to have her around, and I've seen his feelings for her change from deep-seated anger to sometimes frustrated but genuine affection.

"Night, Ron. Night, Mum." Sam kissed her and followed them to the front door, waiting to wave at them as they drove away.

Meg came through to the hallway, sleepily pleased to see us. There was no sign of anxiety or agitation tonight and she just greeted us both, tail wagging slowly, then headed back to bed.

"Go on up, Alice, if you want to. I'll turn everything off down here."

"I will."

"But just one thing…"

"Oh yeah?"

"If you had to pick, me or that Si bloke, who would it be?"

"Sam," I said, "love of my life. That's easy. Si, of course."
I laughed, kissed him, then went upstairs.

"I'll remember that," Sam whispered.

"You should!"

I checked in on Ben, then headed to the bedroom, where
I undressed happily, pleased to have had a good night, and,
although I'd enjoyed them, happy that the parties were
over, and I didn't have to think about them anymore.

After brushing my teeth, I climbed into bed, wondering
what Lydia was doing, and whether she had indeed said
yes to Si this time. I left the light on for Sam, but was fast
asleep before he came upstairs.

13

It is difficult being at home, knowing that up at Amethi one of my favourite events of the year is taking place. But obviously the yoga is out of the question and, now that I've accepted that I need to rest a little more, the slightly uneasy feeling I've had these last few weeks is all but gone.

Ben is in nursery and with Karen on his usual days, and Sam is at work. I have the house to myself, if you don't count Meg. This is incredibly rare, so despite my fear of missing out (FOMO according to Sophie, and to Sam, who thinks he's still cool), I am grateful for this downtime. I can't sit around twiddling my thumbs, though. No daytime TV for me.

I have already worked out a structure to the day – emails and other Amethi admin for two hours. Take Meg down to the beach for a walk (I have caved in and admitted it's best if I drive down there rather than walk all the way and have to heave myself back up the hill). Come back for lunch. Check emails. Pick up Ben. Suddenly, it doesn't seem like I do have a lot of time after all. Plus, there is Christmas to prepare for. Even though we're staying at Mum and Dad's, we will have Sophie with us for the whole of the school break, so I need to make sure her room's ready, and that we have enough food, and I've bought presents for everyone I meant to...

I feel like my heart is beating faster, and I slow this train of thought. *Slow down. Deep breath.*

Relax.

The first day starts well, and I love the chance for some time on the beach with Meg, though it's hard work trudging through the damp sand, and it's windy, so by the time I'm back home, I have sand in my eyes, hair, and everywhere. So does Meg. She also rolled in some seaweed, which had something dubious in it, so she needs a bath. Which eats into my lunchtime, and I abandon that in favour of eating a bowl of soup at my desk. It's not really a good combination, soup and keyboard, and I end up holding the bowl close to my chin and slurping the soup in quickly, as I've seen a message I want to reply to, about milk supplies for new year.

An email springs in from Julie:

Dear Alice Branvall nee Griffiths,

I can see quite clearly that you are online. I hope you're just scrolling through Instagram, and not working. I've told you, I've got it all covered.
The morning has been a resounding success. Everybody loves Lizzie (and me, of course – what's not to love?). Lunch was great (again – me – amazing), and now it's downtime before the afternoon's slooooooow yoga session, which I am going to have to miss to get Zinnie. But don't worry, Luke will be home in time for me to get back up here for dinner.

I told you, everything is under control. Switch off.

With very warm regards,
Your best friend and business partner.
P.S. I mean it. SWITCH OFF.

I smile as I read this. I check the time. It's 1.47. I have to collect Ben at three. Really, there is barely time for anything. But I should listen to Julie. Seize this opportunity. Switch off. I spy another email, from Lizzie.

Dear Alice,

I hope you're having a good day at home. I know you'll be finding it hard to separate yourself from work, and I thought that this might help.
I've been thinking a lot about what you said, about Elizabeth and baby Rose. And I feel guilty for taking you there that day, though it felt like the right thing at the time. But I didn't mean it to cause you undue stress. I knew I wanted to share what happened to Anise with you some day, and I didn't know how, but that set it in motion. So, thank you for listening, as I knew you would. It comes and goes, I've found, and it's all been on my mind a lot since that day. I've felt closer again to Anise lately – and Elizabeth is on my mind a lot as well. Maybe because you've brought her into focus for me. I will be sending up my wishes for them all at the solstice fire, and I'm planning on going back to the beach on Christmas Eve. I will take my lunch, and sit with her, if she's there. I know I sound mad! But it's what I believe. No judgement, eh? I promise we will have the best week at Amethi, and I will let you know if there are any problems. So do not worry. Rest while you can, and don't forget to BREATHE!
Love Lizzie xxxx

There are two audio files attached to the email. I click to download them and open the first. It's Lizzie's voice!

"Hi Alice. I know you'll be missing the yoga this week, and I know you might be finding it hard to relax. So I thought I'd record a couple of meditations for you. One for the daytime, and one for the nights, if you're having trouble sleeping. Do not listen to either of these if you have to be anywhere in the next hour! I'd recommend the daytime one early in the day, maybe once you've got the house to yourself. Anyway, here goes…"

I listen to the first few lines. "Find yourself somewhere comfortable. Your bed… the floor (maybe use a yoga mat for a bit of extra cushioning)… or sit up on the sofa." Lizzie's calm voice makes me smile, and transports me to the many times I've enjoyed listening to Lizzie up in the Mowhay. "Just take a few moments to really relax. Make sure you are fully supported, and comfortable, and baby is comfortable, too…"

There is calm music in the background, which I recognise from Lizzie's yoga sessions, and I close my eyes briefly, imagine I am there. I will be again, all too soon.

With time ticking on, however, I can't do this right now, unfortunately. I press pause, then close the file. I will listen to the night-time one later, and do as Lizzie suggests tomorrow. Maybe I really should just cut out those two hours of work from my daily schedule, and trust in my friends to let me know if there is anything urgent. Julie can access the emails as well, so we won't miss anything.

I feel happy to have allowed myself even more leeway, and I now have about an hour to myself. Meg is fast asleep on the kitchen floor, so I quietly get a glass of water, and head into the lounge. What was I saying about daytime TV? Maybe I can just watch a little bit. *Four in a Bed,* perhaps. That's kind of like research for work.

I have to leave the house on the third episode. I set the TV to record the remaining episodes. So much for no daytime TV. Still, I have to be adaptable, and I'm starting to unwind.

I listen to the night-time meditation, but in the morning I can barely remember any of it. I must have fallen asleep very quickly. Is that Lizzie's intention? What if she is secretly hypnotising me while I sleep? Maybe I'm going to find myself baaing like a sheep when I hear a police car siren, or strutting like a chicken when the phone rings.

I feel good, though. Really good. While Sam is having a shower, I go downstairs with Ben. It's still dark outside, so I keep the lounge curtains closed and switch on the Christmas tree lights and the television. I used to love that, when I was little, sitting with just the lights from the tree.

"You sit here for a bit, I'm going to make eggs for breakfast!" I plonk him on the settee and kiss him on the top of his head, taking a moment to appreciate his soft curls.

Breakfast is usually a rushed affair, as Sam and I both try to get ready for work, while making sure Ben has everything he needs, and we haven't forgotten any kind of special event they're running at nursery, like a themed fancy-dress day (of which there seem to be quite a few), or swimming, or yoga. I love all this stuff, but it's hard work keeping on top of it, and I feel more anxious than I should about forgetting something. I mean, he's two years old. Nevertheless, Julie and I try to remind each other of anything different going on.

Today, though, I feel relaxed, refreshed, and surprisingly light on my feet, considering I really am not light on my feet. I silently thank Lizzie. She can probably sense my gratitude emanating across the town. But I'll make sure I actually tell her when I see her, just in case.

"Breakfast's nearly ready," I call through to the lounge. There is no answer.

"Ben?" I walk through, and I don't see him straight away. I feel an innate moment of panic. Then I spot him, and Meg, their bottoms protruding from the floor-length curtains by the doors into the garden.

"What are you doing, Ben?" I ask, relieved, then suddenly nervous again. What are they looking at?

"Snow," he says.

"Snow?" I cry, delighted, my relief flooding back. I rush over, and push the curtains back. The dark of the night is just cracking open, shards of new daylight filtering through. I rub the top of Meg's head, and she pushes against my hand. She is perfectly relaxed. There is no need for alarm. It's not snowing, though.

"Where's the snow, Ben?"

"It's Christmas," he says. "Snow."

"Ahh, maybe, Ben. Maybe. But it doesn't really snow a lot in Cornwall, you know. Even if it is Christmas." I feel the need to remind him. But this, I know, he does not want to hear.

"I want snow."

"Me too. That would be lovely. But we're going to have a really nice time at Christmas, even if it doesn't snow. And listen, it's Auntie Lizzie's bonfire tomorrow night. Do you want to come to that?"

"No."

"Oh. OK. Maybe you'll feel like it tomorrow."

"No."

"Right, well, anyway, breakfast's ready. Are you coming through? Sam!" I call. "Breakfast!"

"Quite the little housewife, aren't we?" Sam says, coming into the kitchen clothed but with wet hair. He rubs it with a towel and grins at me. "I could get used to this."

"You could, if you were married to somebody else," I say. *"Little housewife,"* I mutter to myself, but I'm smiling too. It actually is a nice feeling, being able to do this in the morning, but for me it's nice because it's the exception, not the norm.

"How are you, Benny?" Sam throws the damp towel over Ben, making him giggle uncontrollably.

"He's been looking for snow, haven't you, Ben?"

"Snow, eh? I'm afraid it doesn't really snow in Cornwall, or not often. Sorry, Ben."

"Maybe we could go to the ice cream farm one day over Christmas," I suggest to Sam.

"That doesn't sound very seasonal."

"Not for the ice cream! They've got a tree, in the middle of the playground, which fires out snow every half an hour."

"Sure. That sounds perfectly normal. Are there little pixies and talking frogs, too?"

"Not real snow, you idiot! And not a real tree! It's part of the playground area, and there's a countdown to this foam shooting out."

"Thank god for that! I thought maybe Lizzie's meditation had turned you a bit mad. Does still sound a bit weird, though."

"I suppose it is. But the kids love it." Julie and I had taken Zinnia and Ben a few weeks back. They'd loved waiting for the beeps that signalled the snow was about to come, though they'd seemed so tiny next to some of the older children, and we'd had to get involved in the snow foam as well. Just to look after our children, you understand. We started throwing the foam at each other, and ended up

109

covered in the stuff. Ben and Zinnia, too young yet to be embarrassed by us, found it hilarious.

I serve up breakfast, giving Meg a small portion of the egg, which she has finished before I've even sat down. She heads towards us, licking her lips.

"No, Meg, you've had yours."

"No, Meg," Ben says, savouring a little bit of authority. His little brother or sister is going to have to watch out, I think.

Meg skulks off to her bed and lies down, head on paws, big brown eyes watching our every move.

"Alright," I say, glancing up at the clock. "You two had better be going in a few minutes."

"I know. I'll just finish these delicious eggs... Probably the best eggs I've ever tasted."

"Flattery will get you everywhere."

"I know."

Once the front door is closed, I listen for the sound of Sam's car leaving the driveway, and then, keeping the curtains closed and Christmas tree lights on, I find the daytime meditation, settle down on the settee, and press play. I listen to Lizzie's introduction and then follow her instructions. I am dimly aware of the sounds of our neighbours heading off to work, and children's voices passing by the front of the house, and then all I can hear is Lizzie's voice. She talks me through tensing and then relaxing every part of my body in turn. Imagining each muscle, each tiny bone. Imagining my baby, deep inside, feeling me unwind, and relaxing, too.

I wake some time later, to a silent house and a dark room. I feel out of place for a few moments, then slowly remember where I am, and what day it is. But the lights of the Christmas tree have turned off.

"Sam?" I call, wondering if he's come back for some reason and switched them off. There is a jingle of a collar and Meg comes trotting through, putting her front paws on the seat, and licking my face.

"Urgh! Meg!" I say. There is no other sound in the house, though. I hope the tree lights aren't broken. Slowly, I pull myself up, and stretch. I guess it's time to open the curtains and acknowledge it's daytime, anyway. As I stand, the tree lights go on again, and Meg looks round at them, her ears pricked up.

"That is weird," I say. We had the electrics redone when we moved in, by Matt, the same guy who looks after Amethi's electrics, so there shouldn't be any issue with them. And you hear all sorts of horror stories about fires caused by Christmas tree lights. Tentatively, I go to the plug socket, and push the switch to off. The lights stay on. What the…? Then ten seconds or so later, they go off.

I open the curtains, happy to see that it's a clear-skied day today. There is even a little sunshine filtering through the trees opposite, the sun not getting quite high enough at this time of year to shine fully on the front of the house. I phone Sam while I open the other curtains, and let Meg out.

"That is weird," Sam says when I tell him what's happened. "God, I hope we haven't got dodgy lights. Tell you what, I'm not taking any chances. I'll get some new ones on the way back from work. Don't turn them back on, will you? I'll switch them over when I get back."

"That's going to be annoying, we'll have to take all the other decorations off as well."

"Better to be safe than sorry, though."

"I guess."

"Don't worry anyway, as long as you're OK. I'd better go, though. Time is money and all that."

"Oh yeah. And I'd better get on with the cleaning. It's not easy being a housewife, you know. A woman's work is never done."

"You'd better not be doing any cleaning!"

"No, I'm going to take Meg out, really."

"Good. Enjoy it. You should get lunch out, too."

"Maybe I will!"

I go to the beach below the station today, and walk with Meg across the sand, to meet the sea. The tide is a long way out right now, allowing passage around to the harbour. I throw Meg's ball, admiring the splash and subsequent small fountain of water. Meg dashes after it, plunging in without a second thought. I just wish I could join her. *Then again*, I think, once I've got my bare feet wet, *maybe not*. It's so cold, it might trigger an early labour.

I watch Meg swim for a little while, then, when she realises I won't be joining her, she returns to shore, sniffing her way along the shallows, creating tiny rainbow splashes in the sunshine. Shoes and socks in hand, I paddle along behind her, trying to ignore the cold which seems to be creeping into my bones. The waves roll gently in and out, foaming a little, but kind and tender today, not reckless and wild.

Turning to face the beach, I look back towards the lifeguard station – unmanned for the winter – and the café, which is all dressed up for Christmas. The sun is almost as high as it will get today, and it glints off windows and skylights across the town, making them glimmer and wink.

My heels sink into the sand as a wave pulls back out to sea. I stop, and feel the same process happen a few times, until my feet are nearly submerged in the sand. Meg has spotted another dog and is loping towards it. I call her back and she comes, never wanting to be too far away.

At the top of the beach, I sit on the wall. It is an effort to put my shoes back on, and I decide not to bother with the socks. Meg and I approach the café, heading to an outside table. It is colder than it has been, but still just about bearable to sit outside, and I don't want to take Meg in anyway. I order a bowl of soup and a bread roll, and the waiter gives Meg a chew, and a bowl of water. She accepts both gratefully.

It was a good idea of Sam's, for me to have lunch out. I sit and savour the soup – pumpkin and red pepper, with just a tiny hit of chilli - tearing up the bread, and dropping lumps in to soak up the soup before I fish them out with my spoon.

From here, I can watch the comings and goings on the beach. It is never empty, but it is so far from the packed-out summer days that it could be an entirely different place. A child and a man come down onto the sand, trying out a kite, while a steady but modest trickle of walkers follows the route from the coastal path and along the shore, disappearing around the rocks towards town, or back the other way. Occasionally, they will break away from this tried and tested route, coming to peruse the menu at the café, or walking past and up the steep slope to the top of town.

The baby fidgets, like it is trying to get comfortable. Perhaps the chilli in the soup is setting it off. Something that feels like an elbow jabs me in the rib cage and I start to feel uncomfortable, too. I finish my soup, and pay the bill. It is nearly one, already, and time to get home before I collect Ben. He is with Karen tomorrow, so I'll have a bit more freedom when it comes to what time I collect him. But then I'll be heading up to Amethi, and joining the solstice celebrations. It's a nice thought.

It seems a shame not to put the tree lights on when we get home, but it would be an even greater shame to have a house fire. I make do with the table lamps, and settle down to watch the rest of yesterday's *Four in a Bed*. I can feel myself getting drowsy, and have to sit up and stretch. It wouldn't do to be late for Ben.

When we're back, I get us both a glass of milk and some coconut rings, and we sit together watching the *Ben and Holly* Christmas special for the five thousandth time.

"See, Mummy? It's snowing," Ben points to the screen.

"Ah, yes, it is in *Ben and Holly* land," I say. "But not here. Not in Cornwall."

He runs to the window, as if to prove me wrong. He returns disappointed.

"Maybe one day, Ben," I say. "But I can tell you what will definitely be happening, and that is Father Christmas coming to visit."

"Here?" he says doubtfully.

"Yes. Well, actually, he'll be coming to the Sail Loft this year. Remember were going to be staying there? Like proper hotel guests! I know you met him at nursery already. But on Christmas Eve, he visits all the children in their homes, and leaves presents for them."

"Not my room," he says.

"Well, no, he doesn't have to come into your room. We'll leave your stocking outside your door, shall we?"

"Put it outside your door. Mummy and Daddy's room."

"OK. We can do that." I realise he doesn't look too happy at the idea of a strange man coming into his bedroom while he's asleep. It's fair enough, really. I know he cried his eyes out at the Father Christmas nursery visit, and he wasn't the only one. "We'll put it outside our bedroom door, and Father Christmas can bring your presents to us. And then in the morning, you can come and open them in our room. Does that sound good?"

"Yes," he nods emphatically, seeming much happier with this scenario.

"And we'll leave a glass of milk and a biscuit for him, shall we?"

"Like we had?"

"Exactly. Or maybe a bourbon. I've heard Father Christmas really likes them. And a carrot for the reindeer."

"Biscuit?"

"No, I don't think biscuits are good for reindeers. They make them sneeze." I pretend-sneeze and Ben falls about laughing. If only everyone was so easily amused.

When Sam gets back, we have tea, and then I put Ben to bed. When I get downstairs, Sam is sitting with a tangle of lights and decorations on the floor.

"Have a fight with the Christmas tree?" I ask.

"Ha, ha. No, I'm just testing these lights out, and the old ones seem fine, but I'll put the new ones on, just in case."

"OK. Come on. You look tired. Let's get this sorted, and have an early night."

Somehow, dressing a Christmas tree for the second time is not as magical as the first time round. We put the lights on, testing them again before adorning the tree with its baubles and tinsel once more. Sam has also bought some chocolate *Ben and Holly* decorations.

"Ben's going to love those!" I exclaim.

"Better hang them out of his reach," says Sam.

"And Meg's."

"Good point."

"And mine."

When it's all done, we stand back to admire our handiwork. I switch off the main lights and we bask in the glow from the tree.

"I think these new lights are better anyway," I say.

"They're exactly the same, Alice."

"The same, but better."

"Sure. Why don't I make us a hot chocolate, and you switch off the lights and get up to bed?"

"I am quite tired," I realise, yawning.

"You're eight months pregnant, Alice, of course you're tired."

"There is that."

Sam goes into the kitchen, and, as I move towards the tree, the lights blink off, then on again. Just for a moment, and I wonder if I've imagined it. But then it happens again.

Sam comes back into the room. I hope he didn't see what just happened, after he's just bought the new lights, and we've spent another hour redoing the tree. But at least if he did, I'll know I'm not going mad. I wonder what it's like decorating a tree for a third time.

"It's happened again," I say, and I turn around. But the room is empty. My skin prickles.

I quickly switch off the lights at the plug and this time they go off straight away, just as they should. Hurrying out of the room, I call to Sam, "I'll just check on Ben," and I scurry upstairs.

Is there something weird going on? Or am I really losing it?

I look in on Ben, then head gratefully to my own bed.

There is always a rational explanation, I hear Sam's voice in my head. I'm not so sure anymore. Or it might depend on your interpretation of the word 'rational'. I decide not to mention the lights to him for now. I'll just hang on, and see what happens tomorrow.

14

The day is already dark when I arrive at Amethi, even though it's not yet five o'clock. The car park is nearly full, and I can hear happy voices coming from the direction of the Mowhay. I have come alone, not even bringing Meg, and I feel a sense of freedom and liberation, having nobody to think about but myself. Well, apart from the paying guests, I remind myself, but having attended the solstice celebrations a few times now, I know there will be a party atmosphere, and nobody's going to be asking for more soap, or wondering if I can book them a taxi into town.

The culmination of a few days of yoga, and often the celebration of new friendships formed, the solstice celebrations are a really wonderful, memorable affair, which Lizzie runs with the minimum of fuss. She lights and tends the fires, gets everybody together, and somehow brings a touch of magic (though she wouldn't call it that).

From a business point of view, we have a tried-and-tested format, beginning with a dinner, and readings from our local writers, Vanessa and Rosie. The Mowhay is glowing with battery-powered tealights and candles, and dressed with generous boughs and wreaths of holly and berries. There is a scent of lemon, ginger and rosemary on the air, along with the fresh, earthy smell of the holly leaves.

I sit next to Lizzie, with Julie on her other side, and I relax in this company of like-minded people – some strangers, some acquaintances, some friends. There is good-natured talk, and a resounding round of applause for Vanessa and Rosie. Lizzie stands to give her usual talk, about the meaning of the solstice, and symbolism of the fire, burning through the night, which will help to honour the return of the light in the morning.

"People think of the summer solstice as the one full of life – and although both winter and summer solstices are, in their own way, about life, the summer actually marks the turn of the earth towards autumn, and winter. The winter solstice, though it comes at a time of year when everything appears dormant, is the point in which we turn towards spring. It may seem a long way off, but it is coming. And deep beneath the earth's surface, there is so much life. So we celebrate in the morning the returning of the light, as the sun rises into the new day. For the earth, this is such an important part of its cycle. For us, it is the perfect time to reflect on the past year, and visualise the months ahead. What do you want from this next year? Think hard on this tonight, and in the morning you can express these wishes, internally, or tell us all if you like! We're listening!"

The room ripples with laughter.

"But for now, I think it's time for rest," says Lizzie. "We have eaten well – thank you, Julie! – and we have wonderful beds for the night. I will be staying by the fire, and any of you will be welcome to join me, but otherwise I will see you in the morning. Early, if not bright. Let's hope for bright though, shall we?"

Julie and I are jubilant as we return to our cars.

"What a job, eh, Alice? What a life!"

"I know. I honestly, truly, can still not believe it sometimes."

"There was something about Lizzie tonight, wasn't there? An extra energy, or something," Julie says. "Oh my god, I'm turning into a right hippy."

"No, I know exactly what you mean. She seemed

more… confident. And I've never thought of her as lacking confidence before."

"Me neither."

"See you tomorrow, Julie. Love you."

"Love you, too, you huge pregnant woman!"

I laugh, and watch as Julie gets into her car and heads straight off. I just want to spend a few moments here, in the dark, and the quiet, and take it all in. The night is clear, and feels almost cold enough for frost, which is a refreshing change. I worry for Lizzie staying out all night, and decide to go back to find her. As it happens, she is on her way to find me.

"Oof!" I nearly bump into her. "Sorry, Lizzie!"

"Alice! I was hoping I'd catch you."

"And I was coming to find you! I just wanted to say, if you get cold, or just want a bed, you can always sleep in my old place – you know, the little cottage, where Jon and Janie lived."

It has lain empty since they left, and Julie and I are still not quite sure what to do with it. As it has a covenant on it that specifies it must be a residence rather than a holiday let, we can't rent it out as we do the other properties. And we can't have just anyone living there, as we have our paying guests to think of. Maybe that is something we need to try and turn around next year. I make a mental note of it, for tomorrow morning, in case I can't think of any wishes. That seems unlikely, somehow.

"Thank you, Alice. I am sure I'll be OK. But I do appreciate it."

"What did you want to see me about?"

"Oh, I just wanted to thank you. For giving me the chance to do all this." She looks like she wants to say more, and I could swear her eyes are shining with tears.

"Lizzie, honestly, it's my pleasure. And Julie's. We were just saying how brilliant you are."

We hug, and I feel an absolute warmth for this woman.

"See you in the morning, Alice," she says.

"See you, Lizzie. And if you should fall asleep in one of those warm, cosy beds, I'll come and wake you up."

"No chance! Go easy, now."

"I will."

I take my time as I walk back to the car, hearing the faintest of breezes amid the few remaining crinkled leaves that cling to the hedgerows and trees. An owl calls, close by. I listen, to hear if the call is answered, and there it is. A little further away than the first one. It feels right, somehow.

I climb into the car and adjust my seatbelt so it's above and below my bump. "Oh, I can't wait to meet you," I whisper to my unborn child. I'm so happy, I could almost cry. Which is ridiculous, I know. But sometimes it hits me, just how good life can be, and I never want to lose sight of how fortunate I am. I turn on the engine and drive towards home, under the clear, star-strewn sky, back to my husband and son.

❄ ❄ ❄

In the morning, I am up in the dark, tiptoeing about the house so as not to wake Sam and Ben if I can possibly help it. Meg looks up, puzzled by the early disturbance. "Go back to sleep, girl," I say. "I'll be back in a bit."

Outside, the streetlights illuminate the first frost of this winter. I am pleased to see it, and it sparkles alluringly on the pavements and across flower beds and front lawns. It is not cold enough that I'm worried about icy roads, but I'm glad I've brought my big coat, and I hope that Lizzie did change her mind and stay in the little cottage. I know she won't have, though. She's made of strong stuff, is Lizzie. Much stronger than me.

The moon is still a presence, keeping watch as I drive along the empty lanes. I glance up at it, and notice a couple of the brighter stars, too. I may not have wanted to wake up when my alarm went off, but I am glad I've not missed this.

When I arrive at Amethi, I feel excited. I can hear the crackling of the fire, and murmur of voices. More subdued than last night, I think, but in a thoughtful, reverent way.

Julie is not yet here, but I make out Lizzie's shape, silhouetted by the fire. She is wearing her poncho; a familiar sight from previous years, and it creates a kind of fuzzy glow around her, like a whole-body halo.

"Alice, you're here!" she greets me, and the two men she's talking to turn and smile.

I think it's the warmth at these gatherings that brings people back to them. The friendliness, and genuine love for each other, and the natural world. It is a difficult thing to achieve, and very hard to replicate. There are not enough occasions when it's possible to feel like this. When strangers welcome you gladly, and genuinely. I feel like I belong.

Julie is with us shortly, as are the last couple of yogis, and the dark sky is already beginning to give in to the pressure of the sun rising in the east. A muted but definite light that was not there just minutes earlier.

Lizzie shakes her tambourine gently, to gain our attention. "Welcome, friends," she smiles around the group. "You are all welcome, and I am so glad you're here to celebrate this special occasion. Some of you are new, some of you have been here before, and some of you," she grins at Julie and me, "practically live here."

The others turn and smile at me and my friend, and I feel shy, but pleased.

"Over the next hour or two," Lizzie says, "we will see the sun take its place in the sky, opposite the moon, which will still be visible for some time today. As we turn our faces to the sun, we will ask the spirits to join us as we welcome it and the new light that it brings. Every time the sun rises, each and every day, the rays that bless the earth, and kiss our skin, are new. Unique. Never seen before, and will never be seen again. Like every breath we take, and every moment we live. So we can look back on our lives to date, and know that we do not need to repeat mistakes. They are in the past, and they can stay there. As the sun's light falls across our skin, we think of the here and now, and of the future. Let its warmth in, let its light bring positivity. Warmth and light are powerful things."

She is going on longer than usual, I think, and I want to glance at Julie, but I don't. I can just see her out of the corner of my eye, and she's watching Lizzie intently. I do the same.

"Let us all go forward into this year with warmth and light, and see what they might bring to us, and our loved ones. Now, if you please, we can form a circle around this fire. The light which has burned all night. And we can begin." She moves on to more familiar ground, "This is the longest night of the year. Now is the time to celebrate the returning of the light. To gather with loved ones and welcome back the sun."

As Lizzie conducts the ceremony, with the incense and the candles, I stay quiet and watchful. I close my eyes as Lizzie passes with the incense, and I try, again, to work out what I can feel. I really do want this connection, to something. The past? The universe? I know it sounds fanciful. I'm self-conscious just thinking these things. I would never say them to Julie, or perhaps even rational Sam. I would say them to Lizzie, though, and I know she'd understand exactly what I mean. She said herself, she has come to this point through her own search, triggered by losing Anise. Maybe it's an innate desire for meaning. Some have religion, ready-made and mapped out. It is not for me, and I am determined to try and find my own way of making sense of things. I just feel that there is more to life than what we humans know. And why shouldn't there be? There is always a rational explanation, Sam says, and I know where he's coming from. He is not closed-minded, but he is incredibly grounded. Not to mention a bit of a science geek. But while I know we understand an awful lot, I'm not sure that it is rational to think that we are all there is. It seems kind of arrogant, in fact, to assume that we're top of the tree.

I listen to the sounds of Amethi as night gives way to day. The tiniest rustling of a small, unseen creature in the rough stubble of the nearby field. Dogs barking at a neighbouring farm, and a cockerel proudly announcing its existence to the world. An owl calling from the line of trees that form the boundary of this special place.

The baby moves, and I feel like something has sighed inside me. I am awash with contentment, and I'm tingling, and I do not want to move, or for this feeling to end. Lizzie smiles at me, and nods. "It is time to invite the spirits to join us, before we turn, as one, to watch the sun rise."

We do as we are instructed by Lizzie, turning slowly from east to south to west to north, returning to face the east, where the sun is following its predestined course. Preceded now by dramatic streaks of light, which make the frost on the ground twinkle like a thin, crisp sheet of glitter.

When it comes to the time to write down our wishes, I know what to write. Not anything for me, or even my family.

Bring peace to Lizzie, and her little girl.

I hold back a little sob as I fold up the paper. I'm hormonal, OK? But I've also been moved beyond words by knowing what Lizzie has been through. And I don't suppose I can ever imagine it. Not really. Despite Lizzie's concern, I don't worry that the same thing will happen to me. What will be will be, and no other person's experience is going to affect that. To think otherwise would be bordering on superstitious, and that is not something I can ever be.

We take it in turns to feed our wishes to the flames; see them rise to the sky, to be received by whatever, whoever, or just evaporate into nothingness. What matters, I realise, is that we have acknowledged those thoughts.

With the sun firmly in place, and our guests tucking into warm bread and mugs of tea or coffee, I seek Lizzie out.

"That was fantastic," I say. "Thank you so much, Lizzie."

"It was my pleasure entirely. You're glowing, Alice."

"Am I? I feel like I am," I admit. "I just… something happened, back there."

"I know. I saw."

"You did? What did you see?"

"It was…"

"Lizzie!" Stewart, one of the newbies this year, comes up, his arms open wide. "That was so… amazing."

I smile. "It was, wasn't it?"

"And do you know how well she's looked after us this week? We haven't wanted for anything."

"She's made not being here very easy for me," I say. "She'll have me out of a job soon," I laugh.

"I didn't mean that. I can see you're... otherwise engaged!" he says, briefly putting a friendly hand on my shoulder. "Blessings on you and the little one."

"Thank you," I say. His partner, Gary, comes up, and soon Lizzie is engaged in a deep conversation about rituals and symbolism, and suddenly I am exhausted.

"I'm going to get going," I tell the three of them, and Lizzie smiles apologetically. 'Don't worry!' I mouth.

I say goodbye and thank you to all our guests, then walk to the car park with Julie.

"Do I need to worry about you, Griffiths?" Julie asks.

"What do you mean?"

"I saw you. Getting all into the solstice shit. Am I going to have another Lizzie on my hands?"

"Would it be so bad if you did?"

"Well, no. But Lizzie's Lizzie, and you're... you!"

"And I always will be," I reassure her. "You know I just love all of this. And always have."

"True," she admits. "OK. I'll let you off. Now get back to that delightfully empty house, and get some sleep."

"I might just do that."

"I'll see everyone off, then close up shop till tomorrow. Then it's Christmas, baby!"

"Bloody hell! It's Christmas."

"Nearly. Today it's no man's land, OK? Make the most of it."

"I will." I hug her, then get in the car and drive home, the winter sun bathing even the barest, brownest of hedgerows, trees and fields with warmth and light.

15

It is Christmas Eve! We've made it through (or near enough).

Yesterday, Amethi was a hive of happy activity, with Julie, Cindy and I working our way around the houses, making them sparkle. On the outside, we hung fairy lights, stringing them along the lengths of the buildings, and hooked a holly wreath from the solstice celebrations on each door. In each lounge, we put up fake trees, all of which needed decorating. We sent frosted fake mistletoe garlands tumbling down the banisters, and put a festive welcome hamper, containing tea, coffee, fudge, biscuits, and a bottle of wine, in every kitchen.

Julie left Cindy and me to decorate the trees while she received the food deliveries for the Christmas catering, and checked she had everything she needed. She returned looking happy, with a menu to sign off, then design and print.

"I'll set it out and print it," I told her, after we'd gone through it all and checked for food allergies and so on.

"Are you sure?" she asked.

"Yes! Don't pretend that wasn't your intention all along."

"Oh, you're just so much better than me, Alice!" she grinned.

"Your charm won't work on me, my friend. But I don't mind. You know I love that kind of stuff."

So I'd gone up to the quiet office, opened my laptop, and found a suitably Christmassy background for the menu. Then I started to type, trying not to feel hungry.

Canapes
Blini with Cornish cream cheese and cucumber. With or without smoked salmon
Bruschetta with Cornish mozzarella, piccolini tomatoes, and basil leaves, drizzled with chilli olive oil
Chilli cashew nuts
Garlic-stuffed olives

Starters
Avocado on granary toast, with chilli olive oil
OR
Breaded mozzarella with cranberry sauce, served with a small salad

Main Course
Lemon garlic salmon
With lemon butter sauce
OR
Mushroom Wellington
Accompanied by our chef's finest vegetarian gravy (even meat-eaters won't be able to tell the difference).

Served with roast potatoes and seasonal vegetables, locally sourced.

Palate Cleanser
Home-made lemon sorbet.

Dessert
Sensational Sticky Toffee Pudding
OR
Beautiful Baked Cheesecake

Served with Cornish cream

Coffee, Tea and Mints to finish

A Cornish cheeseboard, local artisan crackers and chutneys and pickles will be available for the evening

Even though Julie's already told me what she's cooking, I was still struck by how much she was going to have to do, single-handed, although I know that she'll more than manage. And the extra fee for all this is going straight to her, although she has no idea about that yet. It's her Christmas Day that she's missing, and I am contributing nothing.

I know she'll love it, though. I'm just concerned about all the washing up, but she says Luke, Zinnie and Cherry are coming to help.

"That's what family's all about, isn't it?"

"Well… I guess. But I am going to feel really guilty, sitting at the Sail Loft, being waited on hand and foot, while you're doing all this."

"No you're not!"

"No, you're right. I'm not. Well, only a little bit."

I set to work, making the menu look pretty, then printing it out and putting it into the fancy folders we use for special occasions.

By the time the sun was setting, we were all shattered, but Amethi was looking amazing. Just for a moment, we left the lights on in all the rooms, and turned on the outside fairy lights, then stood back to admire our handiwork. The effect was wintry, warm, and welcoming. It made me think of a ski resort, without the snow. I took some shots of it all, with the Christmas tree in the forefront. Then Julie photographed all the interiors, for our own sense of pride, and to add to our social media. Shona will be pleased.

I will leave posting any pictures until after the guests have arrived, though, as they should be first to see it all. I love the thought of them turning up here, tired after their journeys, to be greeted by this festive scene. I imagine being one of them: stepping out of the car, stretching achy limbs, then rounding the corner from the car park to see the twinkling lights and glowing windows of their holiday homes, and knowing that Christmas has truly begun.

Earlier in the day, Sam had gone up to Devon to collect Sophie. I had been looking forward to an evening with them and Ben, but when I got home, the house was empty. The phone started ringing the moment I stepped through the door.

"Hi Alice," it was Sam, and he was sounding merry.

"Hello?" I said tentatively, wondering why he was using the landline. He never does that. I know I am always still a little bit on edge after his accident. Part of me is expecting the worst, though I am trying to fight this feeling, knowing it's irrational, really. "Why aren't you calling my mobile?"

"I did, only about a million times. There was no answer."

"Oh. Sorry," I said sheepishly. I'd had it on silent, and forgotten to turn the sound back on, and to check it.

"Anyway, what I wanted to say was…"

"You love me and you're so glad you married me?"

"Well, yes! Obviously. But also," he said, an apology in his voice, "Kate and Isaac asked me to stay tonight. I didn't think you'd mind. I know you're really busy, anyway. The only thing is, I won't be there to have Ben in the morning, when you're at Amethi. I was going to ask Mum…"

"Oh. OK." My mind started whirring. The plan had been for Sophie and Sam to return in the late afternoon, collecting Ben from Karen's. We were going to get a takeaway, and then in the morning they would take Ben and Meg to the beach if the weather was OK, while I came to Amethi to welcome our guests. Usually, we don't allow people in until the afternoon, but as it's Christmas Eve, and we had Friday to sort the place out anyway, this seemed like the best idea. It also meant Julie and I could spend some time with our families. Anyway, no big deal. "Don't worry about asking your mum. I'll just bring Ben to Amethi with me. And of course you should have a night up there with Kate and Isaac. You've hardly seen them this year."

"Are you sure you don't mind?"

"Sam," I said, "I can already tell you've had a drink! But no, I don't mind at all. Honestly. Have a great time."

"You are amazing, and I am so glad I married you."

"I know."

At least I hadn't taken off my boots and coat. I called Karen and told her I was on my way to get Ben. Ron arrived at the same time as me.

"Well, hello, Alice. My, you've grown," his eyes twinkled mischievously. "Sorry, you're not meant to comment on a lady's size, are you?"

"Yes, how rude of you, Ron." I smile. "And luckily I'm not a lady, so it's not a problem."

He roared with laughter. I like making him laugh, and I feel he's much too generous with it for my attempts at humour, but still, it makes me feel good.

"Come to get little Benesek, is it? He's a good boy. Makes his granny very happy, too."

"Well, he loves her. And I am so grateful for her help. Sam, too."

Ron turned his face to the sky. "New front coming in, Alice."

"Is there?" I asked, trying to sound like I knew what that meant.

"Yep. Might start to feel like winter soon."

"Well, I think that would be good. I'd rather have some proper weather. It doesn't seem right to have had such a warm December."

"No, I agree. I remember winters when I was a boy. Proper cold, they were. The frost'd get in the windows, creep across the glass inside. Bloody hell, I sound old, don't I?"

"More cold than old," I said, and he roared again.

"Speaking of which, let's get you inside," he said, brandishing his key.

"Mummy! Grandad Ron!" Ben shouted, running to us, his face a mess of tomato sauce.

"Ben, let me guess what you've had for tea. Is it beans?" Ron asked.

"Yes!"

"I haven't had a chance to wipe his face yet. Sorry, Alice," Karen came smiling into the hallway.

"It's not a problem at all," I said, lifting Ben to me and emitting a groan as I did so.

"You want to be careful, lifting great big weights like this," Ron tickled Ben, producing some pleasing giggles, "in your condition."

"I can't really avoid it," I said. "And anyway, I don't want to. I'm fine. Mummy's strong, isn't she, Ben?"

"Yep!" he said, squeezing my head between his arms in a tight cuddle.

"But I can't breathe!" I laughed, and he loosened his grip.

"I hear Sam's got a night in Devon, then?" Karen asked.

"That's right."

"It's so lovely, the way you young folk all get on. She's not a bad girl, Kate, is she?"

"She's great. Honestly. And she seems so happy now. Sophie, too."

"I know. I can't wait to see her. She changes every time. So grown up."

"She really is."

132

"Do you want a cuppa, Alice?"

"I won't, if you don't mind. It's been a long day, and I need to get this one back, and into bed. It's possible we may not get a lot of sleep tomorrow night!"

"Is Santa coming to see you then, Ben? Have you been a good boy?" Karen asked her grandson, wiping his face with a warm wet cloth she'd brought through from the kitchen, then kissing his cheek.

"Yes! Yes!" Ben wriggled, trying to escape the cloth.

"Well, that's good then, isn't it?"

"Right. Thank you, Karen," I said, as Ron handed me Ben's bag. "I'll see you at the Sail Loft on Christmas Day!"

"We can't wait, can we, Ron?"

"We can't," he agreed, kissing Karen on the cheek and putting his arm round her shoulder. "I have a feeling it's going to be an extra special Christmas this year."

"I hope so," I smiled, and carried Ben to the car. My back was aching a bit. It crossed my mind that perhaps I should take Ron's advice. But how could I not pick up my two-year-old boy? It would be impossible.

I was so glad Karen had done Ben's tea. All I had to do was give him a bath, and get him to bed.

Ben came upstairs with me, while I ran his bath. "Nearly ready, Ben," I called, going through to his room. He was on his chest of drawers, looking out of the window.

"What have I said about climbing up there?" I said sternly. He can't open the window himself, but even so, it makes me nervous.

He just grinned at me. "Snow, Mummy!"

Not this again. I peered out, pressing my face to the glass so I can see. "No snow, Benny."

Our next-door-neighbour, Diane, was just arriving back from work. We waved to her, then I pulled the curtains to, helped Ben undress, and got him in the bath. I covered his hair and chin with bubbles and showed him in the mirror. "Look, you're Father Christmas!" Then we pretended the bubbles were snow, throwing handfuls at each other. I ended up soaked, which was just the excuse I needed to put my own pyjamas on, after Ben was in his.

Warm and toasty in his bed, I put on his star light and read to him, and he was asleep within minutes. All this Christmas stuff is exhausting, I know. I realised I was kind of glad, in the nicest possible way, that Sam and Sophie had stayed in Devon. I had a whole, luxurious evening to myself. Selecting *Bridget Jones' Diary* as a suitably easy, cheesy, sort-of-seasonal film to watch, I ordered a curry, and poppadoms, pickles, and a veggie samosa, and got a mug of hot water, with a slice of lemon. Then I put on the Christmas tree lights, turned off the others, and settled down to the film.

After ten minutes, the Christmas tree lights went off. I stood, sighing, moved towards the tree, and the lights came back on again.

"Bloody hell," I muttered. "Not this again." Just when I was properly relaxing. I sat back down. The lights went off again. Then the TV. I was plunged into darkness. I heard Meg's collar jingling and her claws on the kitchen floor. Then she was at my side, pushing into me.

"It's OK, Meg. Must be a power cut." But the hallway light was on. I could see it filtering into the room, under the door. I felt cold, suddenly. "It's OK," I said again, more to reassure myself than Meg. I stood and headed to the light switch, trying the main lights, but the room stayed stubbornly dark, so I opened the door to the hallway and then there was a loud knock on the door. I shrieked, and nearly jumped out of my skin.

"The takeaway, Alice," I reprimanded myself for being so silly. Of course, it was just the takeaway. Holding Meg's collar, and trying to look calm and composed, I answered the door to the smiling delivery man, and gratefully took the food. Seeing the outside world, so normal and every-day, made me feel better. It might be dark, but it was still early evening. Perhaps there was something wrong with the electric circuit for the lounge, I told myself, not even knowing if that was a thing. I closed the door, turned back into the hall, and saw that now all the tree lights were back on, and the TV, too. Meg went in ahead of me, calmer now, and sniffing around, then settled down in front of the settee emitting a deep-felt sigh.

I laid out the food on the coffee table and brought in a plate and cutlery, closing the kitchen blinds while I was in there, found the film once more, and started it again, from the beginning. The aroma of the curry made my mouth water, and I was soon tucking in, as though nothing untoward had happened. But I kept the door to the hallway open – and put the chain on the front door, too. Just in case.

After I'd finished my food, I cleared away the detritus and continued with the film, soon relaxing enough to curl up on the settee, and actually let my muscles and mind unwind. I know this film so well, all the way through to the final scene, when Bridget's in her pants, vest and cardigan, in the snow, and Mark Darcy is kissing her. It is romantic, I suppose, but, ever practical, I always think I'd have got fully dressed before dashing out into the cold, snowy, London night. I suppose taking ten minutes to pull on thermals, leggings, jeans and a jumper – finishing with hat, scarf, and gloves - might ruin the moment, though.

At bedtime, I let Meg into the garden, reminding myself that there was nothing to fear, then I checked all the doors and windows, and left the hallway light on when I went upstairs. I wasn't scared, exactly, but I was very aware that it was just me, Ben and Meg in the house. Before I closed my bedroom curtains, I made myself open the window for a while, look outside, and remember where I was. I could hear loud music from the town, and the sounds of people shouting, but in a friendly, good-natured way. It was good to remember I was part of something, and not isolated. Just a few minutes away, should I need them, were Mum and Dad, and Karen and Ron – and Julie and Luke. I closed the window, pulling my curtains to, then getting into bed. Luckily, sleep didn't take long to come, and when I woke up, it was to Ben bouncing on my bed.

"Christmas, Mummy! Snow!"

"Are you sure?" I opened an eye suspiciously. There was none of the glow of white that I would expect if the outside world was snow-covered. In fact, it just looked dark.

"Open the curtains, Ben. Let's see…" I pushed myself up with my elbows, buying a little time to wake fully while my boy ran to the window. He pulled back the curtains to… darkness. No surprise to me, but apparently a crushing disappointment to him.

"Don't worry, Benny. It might not snow, but we're going to have so much fun, with Daddy and Sophie, and Nanny and Grandpa, and Granny and Grandad Ron. And don't forget Father Christmas is coming tonight…" The look of terror on Ben's face as I uttered these last words made me instantly regret them. "But we'll put your stocking by Mummy and Daddy's door, shall we? And I tell you what, when we leave a message for Santa, I'll put a special note asking him not to go into your room, shall I?"

He nodded firmly, his mouth a straight line. His hair was messy from sleep, and one of his pyjama legs halfway up his calf. "Come and have a cuddle, Ben! Before we have to get dressed."

"*Ben and Holly?*"

"Not right now," I inwardly groaned. "We can put it on downstairs while Mummy gets breakfast ready, OK?"

"OK."

❄ ❄ ❄

Julie picks us up, to go to Amethi. As we wait for her to arrive, I have Ben in one arm, perched on my hip, and Meg on her lead in my other hand. The plan had been for just me and her to go but I see immediately that she has Zinnia in her car seat.

"Snap!" I say. "Looks like it's the four of us, then! I meant to tell you I've got Ben. Sam decided to stay in Devon for the night. He did call yesterday, more than once, but by the time I spoke to him, I'd say he was a little bit sozzled, so there was no way he was coming back."

"And Luke's got work to do. I know we do, too," she says apologetically, "but he's got video calls and all sorts, and I can tell you from experience that video calls and that little one do not mix. He's got to get Jim to the doctor's, too."

"Is everything OK?"

"I think so. Maybe a UTI, I think. But I insisted they go today. Jim doesn't want to get stuck with one of them over Christmas. They can get nasty. He's feeling pretty rough as it is, which is why Luke said he'd take him."

"Well, now these two can hang out together, and tire each other out. It's going to be a great day!"

I'm happy to let Julie drive and I sit back, taking in the

bare hedgerows, the sleeping fields, and the sky, which opens ahead of us as the land flattens just outside the town. It is all clouds again this morning, and determined to keep us separated from the sun.

While Ben and Zinnia follow us around, and Meg trots off for some peace and quiet, we set to work going round the cottages, double-checking everything. Julie deposits a basket of wood for the fires in each house.

"It all looks so cosy!" I say delightedly. "I wish we were staying ourselves."

"I know! Maybe we should do that one year."

We stop for a break, and take our mugs to sit outside the Mowhay. Julie's whipped up hot chocolate with all the trimmings, and it's going down a bit too well. I wipe a little cream off the tip of my nose, while Ben, Zinnia and Meg chase each other round and round the table where we're sitting.

"Stop it, you lot! You're making me dizzy!" I laugh.

The clouds have crept slightly closer while we haven't been watching.

"If I didn't know better, I'd say they look like snow clouds," Julie says.

"Snow?" Ben looks round sharply.

"No, Ben, sorry. Not snow clouds. Auntie Julie was just saying they look like them. But it's not going to snow today. Which is good, isn't it?" I add brightly. "Because Daddy and Sophie are coming home!"

"Sophie!" Ben yells, running past Zinnia, who copies him. She might have taken a while learning to walk, but she's certainly made up for it. Meg dances around them, panting, knowing they are too small to jump on, but desperate not to miss out.

I take a look at the sky. I can see what Julie means. There is that kind of purplish tinge there that I always associate with snow. And the air has retained its night-time cold today. It does feel like winter, at last.

"Come on, kids. Come and have your drinks while they're still hot, then we can wait for the guests to arrive, and…"

I stop, distracted. I'm sure that was a snowflake, drifting gently down in front of me. I look at Julie, and see that it is not the only one. Slowly, slowly, more arrive, gliding softly to earth.

"No way!" Julie cries, smiling widely. "Christmas snow!"

"Snow!" shouts Ben. "Christmas!"

"Yes, it is snowing, but don't expect too much, Ben. It might just be a few flakes. Aren't they beautiful, though?"

We sit for a few moments, while the snow shower passes. The air is quiet, and calm. Even the chattering jackdaws are still. I let myself imagine a proper blanket of snow up here. And a white Christmas! I don't think I have ever had one, but I remember longing for it when I was a child, so I know how Ben feels.

"Come on," I say reluctantly. "There's work to do."

"There is."

We settle the kids down at the Mowhay table, with Christmas colouring sheets – snowmen and Christmas trees and presents, and even that terrifying intruder, Father Christmas.

I hear the office phone go. "Damn, I should have brought it down here."

"Don't worry, I'll get it." Julie runs off and I stand by the bifold doors. The sky is unmistakeably darker, but the snowflakes have dried up. I hope it's not going to rain. That would put a dampener on proceedings, literally.

I hear Julie's voice, then her running down the steps, two at a time.

"They can't make it, Alice. They're stuck in snow!" Sam and Sophie spring to mind. My face falls. "The Shropshire guys, I mean. The Coopers," she goes on, and I am instantly relieved. "Apparently, it's been really heavy up there, and the roads are awful around them. They've decided it's too far to travel. They're so gutted."

"Oh no, that's awful." I do feel bad for them, but the business side of me is also thinking about the piles of food we have bought, not to mention the money the Coopers have paid for their holiday. We have never had this situation before, and I don't know if it's going to be up to us to refund them. Surely holiday insurance is for just this kind of eventuality, though? If they have it. What if they don't? I'd feel awful taking their money for a holiday that hasn't happened.

Julie is fiddling with her phone. She puts on a radio station. "We should get the weather forecast soon," she says.

As it happens, we don't have to wait for the forecast. The surprise weather is the main news headline. "Roads across the country have been covered by this unexpectedly heavy snowfall, with motorists left stranded. The north-west of the country, and the Midlands, have suffered the worst so far, with even the M6 and M5 brought to a standstill. The snow-storm is expected to move south and west and cover much of England over the course of the day. Police are warning people not to travel unless absolutely necessary."

My heart is pounding. I reach straight for my phone, to speak to Sam. Luckily, Devon wasn't mentioned, and I'm hopeful he and Sophie will be well on their way by now anyway. He said they'd be leaving after breakfast. I get his voicemail, as he normally switches his phone off when he's driving. I try Sophie, too, and get her voicemail as well. I message them both.

We've just heard about the snow upcountry... hopefully not in Devon. Are you both OK and on your way? Hurry up, just in case we get it here! xxx

"Let's see what else we can find out," says Julie. "Hopefully the others are going to make it down here. Where are they coming from, again?"

"Erm... Taunton and, I think, Gloucestershire?" I say, walking back to the window. "I hate to say it, but it does look pretty overcast here. I wonder how far down the country it's got."

"Fingers crossed not as far as Devon," she says.

"Don't even..." The thought of Sam and Sophie stuck in the snow for Christmas is not one I want to contemplate. I've seen images on TV of drivers stranded in their cars, having set off on journeys not really believing that they could get stuck. It's one of those things you always think won't happen to you, and we're so unused to snow in this country, I don't think any of us would be prepared for it.

"God, it's definitely trying here," Julie says quietly, so as not to alert the kids, and nudges me. There are proper flakes coming down again – bigger than the last lot. Meg is lying under one of the tables, looking up at the sky.

"Perhaps we should cover the outside furniture," I say. "Just in case."

"We should phone the Browns and the Barretts, too. Make sure their journeys are going OK."

While Julie calls our expected guests, I sit on one of the seats just inside the door and watch keenly, as the snowflakes continue to fall. I check my phone. Nothing from Sam and Sophie, but then it looks like my signal's a bit dodgy at the moment. It can be patchy up here sometimes. I'll try them from the office phone after Julie's finished with it.

"I see," says Julie, as she walks into the room with the phone to her ear. "No, I completely understand. I think I'd come to the same conclusion. It's very wise. And yes, maybe you'll be able to get down here when this snow clears, and enjoy the rest of your week down here anyway … I know, it's so disappointing. I'm so sorry … No, no, nothing any of us could do about this!"

She ends the call and looks at me. "Two down, one to go."

"That was the Browns?"

"Yes, they didn't want to risk the journey. It's quite a trek from Gloucester, and they said it's snowing quite a lot near them. They didn't want to get part of the way, and then realise that they're stuck in the middle of nowhere."

"Bloody hell, what a nightmare! Shall I try the Barretts?"

"Yeah, OK. Here's their numbers. I'd better phone Mum, too. I have a horrible feeling she won't be coming, either." Julie hands me a post-it with two scribbled mobile numbers. She takes her phone, while I try both numbers in turn. Both go to voicemail, and I leave messages asking them to call back to let us know they're OK, and on their way (or not). If they can make it from Somerset, then there is hope for Sam and Sophie, who have less of a journey from Devon. They're really not that far from the border with Cornwall, so I'm hopeful they will be well on their way by now.

I try Sam and Sophie again, from the landline this time, but again receive no response. I am starting to panic a little, and I want to reach for my blood pressure monitor, but I bear in mind Sandi's advice, and I leave it be.

They'll be fine, I tell myself. But the snow is showing no sign of stopping, and here and there it looks like it's starting to stick.

"Did you manage to speak to Cherry?" I ask Julie when she comes back in.

"Yes," she says, "and she's stuck, too. She said she went to the supermarket this morning for some last-minute things and by the time she got outside, the snow was already setting. She wanted to wait and see if it clears, but I think she should stay put. No point risking it. At least Lee's just down the road, so she's not totally alone."

"That's a real shame, though. I bet she was looking forward to coming down here."

"Yeah, and she's only got a couple of days off work, so we're going to have to completely postpone. But I'll go up and see her in January, I think. Take Zinnie up to visit. Any luck with the Barretts?"

"No, not yet. Or Sam and Sophie."

"We'll just wait a while," Julie says. "It's only just after ten, I'm sure we'll hear from them soon. As long as we don't get snowed in!" she laughs.

"Snow!" Ben looks up at Julie's words. He swivels his head to the window and his eyes widen with delight. "It's snowing, Mummy!" He runs to the window, and then to me, and puts his arms round one of my legs.

"It really is, Ben," I say. At least one of us is happy about it.

As half an hour passes, then an hour, I start to feel increasingly nervous. There is still no word from Sam, or the Barretts, but Julie has spoken to Luke, and he says it's not too bad in town, so hopefully I'm worrying about nothing.

We keep the radio on, and everybody on air seems very excited about the prospect of a white Christmas.

"I'll take the kids outside, shall I?" Julie suggests.

"They might as well enjoy it," I acknowledge, so we wrap them up in their coats, and I dig out the gloves and hat I've been carrying around for Ben for ages, just in case winter ever showed its face. Well, it certainly has now.

"Too right! We should be out there with them. I love a good snowball fight."

"I'll stay in here and listen out for the phone," I smile.

"Sure. You stay here, and keep warm and dry. I'll take this one for the team!" laughs Julie.

But no phone calls come. I message Sam and Sophie again, and have a sneaky check of my blood pressure, which is slightly higher than normal – in fact, right on the cusp of worrying, but that's not surprising, given the current situation.

Julie doesn't seem overly concerned about the situation, but I don't know whether I should treat that as a comfort or not. Of the two of us, she has always been the more flippant, and light-hearted. It's a great thing in many ways, as she's got me doing things I never would have on my own, including coming back down to Cornwall. But on the other hand, maybe sometimes it would be better if she took things a bit more seriously. In this situation, I just don't know whether I should take the lead more, or let Julie's more positive, laidback attitude seep into me.

I'm worried about Sam and Sophie, travelling in the snow, and the situation is entirely out of my control. There is literally nothing I can do. My gut feeling is that we should get back to town now, but then what about the

Barretts? They can't turn up to find nobody is here.

"What do you think, Julie?" I call out of the door. I can't help smiling at the sight of the three of them with snow clinging to their clothes, and the children's sparkling eyes and rosy little cheeks, glowing with the cold. "I was going to try the Barretts again. Then maybe we wait another hour? Half an hour? Head back to town? We can always leave the key in their door, if we have to. I know it's not ideal, but it's Christmas. They'll understand."

"OK," Julie says. She knows me well enough to see that I am starting to get agitated. "Good idea, Alice. If you don't mind, why don't you go and lock up the other houses? I'll just finish up here—" she sneaks a gentle snowball Ben's way and he belly laughs, and falls over on purpose "—then I'll pack away as much of the food as I can. We'll have to find a use for it. Maybe the soup kitchen could use it tomorrow. I'll ask Jim later."

"Great idea. No problem, I'll go and lock up."

I am grateful for the gravel paths, keeping me sure and steady as I make my way around to the holiday lets. There is a thin layer of snow now, and I'd hate to slip over. Meg joins me and wanders along at my side. I make her stay outside, with her snow-covered paws, while I pop into each house to check all the electric switches are off, before locking up. All of this feels such a shame, and the houses now seem colder, and lacking in life. Our beautiful holiday lets, so Christmassy and beautiful, and for nothing. But maybe we'll recover it a bit – perhaps the Coopers and the Browns will get down here on Boxing Day, if the snow is short-lived. Perhaps even tomorrow, if they don't mind travelling on Christmas Day. I don't think I'd fancy it, though. As for the Barretts, there is still a chance they'll get here. Then they will have Amethi to themselves for

Christmas. That seems quite an attractive prospect.

At the largest of the holiday lets, I am in the kitchen when I hear Meg's claws on the slate tiles.

"Meg!" I call warningly. "Outside!"

Nothing. I go through to the lounge and there she is, looking straight at the tree, which is lit up – but it shouldn't be. Just moments ago, I had been in and checked all the plug sockets were off in this room. Maybe I accidentally switched that one on, though. Meg starts wagging her tail enthusiastically as I go over to turn the lights off. Only, they're not turned on at the wall. They flicker, and Meg starts barking.

There must be a rational explanation, I tell myself, but my senses are heightened, and I think I can feel something… someone? My heart is racing, and I want to get out of here as quickly as I can, but I make myself stay.

Meg is not scared, I realise, but excited. I don't know what to think. The lights flicker again, then are dark. It's too much. I scurry out of the room, Meg at my heels, and into the snowy outdoors, locking the door behind me. My breath is heavy, and my heart beating wildly.

"Alright?" Julie appears at my side. "I've got some of the food sorted, and the kids are in the car, ready to go."

"Bloody hell! That was quick."

"Not really. You've been gone ages."

"Have I?"

"Yes! I thought maybe Sam had called, or the Barretts."

"No," I say, looking at the phone, in case I'd somehow missed a call.

"Are you OK? You look a bit flustered."

"Oh, yeah, no, I'm fine," I garble.

"Good! Don't worry, everyone will be OK, Alice. It might be some of the mobile masts are affected by the weather. More than likely, in fact. Let's just get home, and we can make a plan from there. You and Ben can come to us if you like, until Sam and Soph get back."

"That would be great," I say. I'm glad Julie has taken my strange behaviour for me worrying about Sam, and it is of course partly that. But I know now that there is something really weird going on, or else I actually am losing my mind. Neither option is very appealing.

❄ ❄ ❄

Julie's car engine is on, and the kids are strapped in their seats in the back. I am grateful not to be driving. I've never really driven in snow before, and I don't want to push my blood pressure any higher.

We manage to get along the driveway successfully, again thanks to the gravel, but we're in for a nasty surprise on the road. The car slides and Julie takes it very easy, but after just a hundred metres or so, the snow seems deeper, and Julie is shaking. Which just goes to show how scary it is, because nothing much puts Julie off her stride.

"I don't think I can do it, Alice," she says. "Shit!" she bangs the steering wheel and turns to look at me, her face as serious as I've ever seen it. "Honestly. I don't... shall I try again?"

I look back at her. "I don't think you should, Julie. If it's like this all the way, we're going to end up stuck in the middle of nowhere. I know it's only a couple of miles to town, but I don't fancy it with these two in tow, do you?"

"No, not to mention the small matter of your pregnancy."

"Bugger, bugger, bugger," I say, managing to keep my swearing low-key, given our back seat companions.

"Snow, Mummy! Christmas!" says Ben.

147

"Yes, that's right. It's snowing," I say, looking out at the wintry scene. The air is now a mass of thick, soft, swirling whiteness, and it's hard to see much further than the hedgerows either side of the road. "Come on, kids," I say, turning round with a smile on my face. "Back to Amethi! Just until it stops snowing so much. We'll have our lunch there, shall we?"

"Yeah! Snowball fight!" says Ben.

"Ball fight!" echoes Zinnie.

"We'll see," I say, and I smile at Julie.

"Should I try to drive back to Amethi?" she asks.

"I don't think so. We can manage the walk, can't we? And the car should be safe enough here."

"I think you're right. Wow. Who'd have thought it? Snowed in in Cornwall."

"And on Christmas Eve," I say, dispirited. There would have been a time I'd have found this exciting, but I'm so tired, and we're missing Sam and Sophie and Luke. Maybe if they were all here, it would be different. Or if I even knew that they were OK. But anyway, maybe it will blow over. We'll be back home and laughing at ourselves in time to leave out the cookies and milk for Santa.

"Alice! Thank God!" Sam's relief mirrors how I feel, at the sound of his voice. "Are you OK?"

"I'm fine, thanks," I laugh. "Well, kind of. We appear to be stuck at Amethi."

"You're stuck?" he exclaims. "Where's Ben?"

"Don't worry, he's with me."

"And is he OK?"

"He's fine. We just tried to get back to town, about half an hour ago, but the roads are impassable at the moment. Are you home?"

"No," he says reluctantly. "I'm afraid not. We're still at Kate's."

My stomach drops. "You're not?"

"We are, I'm afraid. I went for a walk with Sophie and Jacob this morning. I know we were meant to head straight off after breakfast, but Kate and Isaac were rushed off their feet, getting ready for their Christmas lot, so I said I'd take Jacob off their hands for a while."

"Right. Isaac and Kate are busy," I say flatly.

Sam sighs. "I know you are too. I'm sorry. We should have set off first thing, and maybe we'd have missed the snow. Now it's coming down really heavy here."

"It is here, too," I sigh. "In fact, our 'Christmas lot' aren't going to be able to get here. Well, maybe apart from one couple, who we haven't heard from yet, but I can't see how they could get to us, even if they can reach town."

"I've got to be honest, Alice, I don't think they'll get that far. And, you know, maybe fate intervened this morning. Perhaps if Sophie and I had left when we'd planned to, we'd be stuck in the snow somewhere in the middle of Cornwall now."

"Maybe," I grudgingly admit. I'm still irritated that he prioritised helping Isaac and Kate out, over coming back here. Especially as Julie and I also have a lot going on at Amethi.

"I'm just so glad to speak to you," he says. "I wasn't sure where you might be, and the home phone's ringing out."

"But you knew I'd be at Amethi, with Ben," I say meaningfully.

"Yes, I did. Sorry," he says again. "I wasn't thinking. Kate and Isaac made me so welcome last night, it seemed the right thing to give them a hand this morning. Don't be mad at me, Alice."

"I'm not." I am. A little. But, more than anything, I'm just gutted. Our Christmas is falling apart before my eyes, and there is nothing I can do about it. "I'd better go. I'll call you later."

"They're still in Devon?" Julie asks after I've hung up.

"Yep."

"It's probably for the best. Imagine if they'd set off and then got stuck somewhere in the middle of Cornwall."

"That's exactly what Sam said. Don't you be so reasonable, you're meant to be on my side!" But I'm smiling.

"Don't worry, Alice, there's still the rest of the day to go. This might all clear, and we can hopefully get back home before tonight. It's only a couple of hours' drive for Sam. It might still come right."

"Yeah, maybe," I say, trying to harness my usual optimism. One look out of the window, however, suggests that the snow is very unlikely to clear any time soon.

"So, what shall we do?" Julie asks, cheerfully. "We're

here right now. You're always telling me to do what Lizzie says – be in the moment. It seems like this is the prime time to try and take her advice. And look. We're in a beautiful place – *our* beautiful place – with our beautiful kids. We've got enough food to feed an army, so I can rustle us up some lunch, and hopefully we won't need to worry about tea here because we'll be home and dry. You'll be at the Sail Loft, with Phil and Sue attending to your every need, and I'll be chilling at home, knowing I don't have to cook a ginormous Christmas dinner tomorrow. Although I'm a bit disappointed, truth be told. I was quite looking forward to it."

"Maybe it will be a Boxing Day feast instead," I suggest, with a little hope.

"That's the spirit!"

"And you're right. We're here now. And Ben's been on about snow for ages. I suppose this is our chance to make the most of it. At least somebody's got their Christmas wish."

"Did you hear that, Benny? You've got a Christmas wish early!"

Ben looks delighted.

"So, should we get out there?" I suggest, lifted suddenly on a wave of seasonal cheer, and feeling a little less hopeless.

"Yes!" Julie says. "What do you think, kids? Shall we go play in the snow?"

"Yes!" they shout back.

When we step outside, I am struck by the absolute quiet that lies beneath the children's excited voices. Meg joins us, stepping carefully at first, trying to get the measure of this deep, cold white stuff, but it's not long before she is bounding, carefree, after the snowballs we throw for her.

"Shall we make a snowman?" I suggest.

"Yes!"

"Or how about a snow family?" Julie says.

"Doggy!" Zinnia shouts.

"And a snow dog," Julie agrees. "Like Meg!" I happen to know Zinnia's Christmas list (dictated to Luke) consists of the word 'dog' and 'ball', and that's it. But apparently 'ball' was only the result of Luke pressing her for more ideas. Essentially, all she wants is a dog, like Meg.

We show the children how to make snowballs and compact them, then begin rolling them across the ground, leaving smooth snow paths in our wake. We pick out the odd bits of gravel which the huge snowballs collect, and soon they are as tall as Ben. "Are these big enough?" I ask.

"No! Bigger!" Ben shouts, throwing snow into the air.

"Bigger!" echoes Zinnie.

I stand and rub my back.

"I'll take it from here," Julie says. "Why don't you get to work on the snow children? And the snow dog?"

She takes the first of the larger balls of snow, which is more like a boulder, and carries on pushing it. It makes a crunching noise with each roll, and she heads towards the Christmas tree with it. "This is the perfect place!" she calls. "And we'll make this the snow daddy. Now for the mummy."

"That's a bit too nuclear family, isn't it?" I laugh. "What would David and Martin say?"

"OK, let's just call them both snow parents."

"Perfect."

She gets to work on the second snow parent, and I roll the smaller snow children bodies over to join the adults. We set them next to each other, showing Ben and Zinnie how to pat extra snow around them until they are smooth and firm, then we get to work on the heads.

"Now we have to give them faces… and maybe hats and scarves, so they don't get cold," says Julie.

"They're made of snow, Julie!" Ben says, sounding very grown-up and disparaging. It makes Julie and me double over with laughter (which isn't easy when you're eight months pregnant). The children join in, though I'm not sure they know why. And in this moment, I feel genuinely, wonderfully happy, remembering what it felt like to be a child in the snow, and swept up in a rush of love for these three people. Making memories – that seems to be a common saying these days, doesn't it? In this instance, I feel that is exactly what we're doing.

I take the kids to my old cottage, where I've stored a few bags of clothes and general bric-a-brac, for the charity shops and eBay, but have never quite got round to sorting yet. There are a few more bags than I'd remembered, as I'd accepted some hand-me-downs from one of the older nursery kid's mums, and left them at the cottage, with every intention of looking through them. I hope I might have time to do these kinds of things when I'm on maternity leave. We find a flat cap, a wide-brimmed straw sun hat, a Peppa Pig woolly hat, a baseball cap, and a couple of patterned scarfs. We get two mismatched socks for the snow dog's ears.

The children carry them back to the snow family, and we begin to dress them.

"I'll go and get some carrots from the kitchen. Maybe some walnuts, for their eyes, seeing as we don't have any coal," says Julie.

"Perfect!"

While the kids fuss around the snow people's clothing, I

stand back and watch them, and take in the wider scene. The snow is still falling steadily, with generous flakes already covering our tracks, and sticking to our clothing, even catching on our eyelashes.

It's a sight to behold, and not one I expect to see again for quite some time, if ever. The world has been muted, it seems. Even the birds are silent, apart from the occasional caw from one of the jackdaws.

The sky is growing darker again, and I'd be hard-pressed to guess the time of day, if I didn't already know it.

"It feels like late afternoon," I say, as Julie returns.

"I know what you mean," she says. "That sky's definitely getting darker. Here, let's get this lot sorted, then head indoors, shall we? It's about lunchtime."

She unloads satsumas, carrots and walnuts onto the snow, and we pick them out, embedding them in the snow people's faces.

"They need smiles," I say, as the satsumas make round Os, as though they are all shocked.

"Maybe they're carol singers?" Julie suggests. "It's going to be difficult to find sticks under all this snow."

I stand back and admire our handiwork. "Carol singers it is. A modern family of non-gender-specific carol singers. Or perhaps festive singers, to keep it strictly secular."

"Holiday singers!" Julie suggests.

"Perfect. We're there!"

I delve inside my coat, to find my phone. "We need to get some photos before we go in."

"Hang on!" Julie says. "I've got an idea."

She disappears around the corner, towards the Mowhay. Even though it's not even lunchtime, the sky is so weighed down with snow, and the air so thick with it, that the day is dim, almost like we are already heading into night. All

154

of a sudden, the strings of lights which adorn all the buildings flick on. The effect is enchanting.

"Look, kids!" I say. "Christmas magic!"

I hug them close to me. Zinnia's cheeks feel cold. "Come on, Julie!" I call. "Let's get some photos, then get these two inside. And me. I'm cold, too." Meg pushes against me. "And Meg!"

We set the phone on timer mode, and manage to get some group photos of us with our secular snow singers, then I take a more pictures, turning 360 degrees to get the full effect, before Julie pulls me.

"Enough, Griffiths! You can always take more later."

We go into the Mowhay, shaking the snow off our boots, and stripping off our hats, gloves and coats, all of which are soaking.

"You know what?" Julie says, as I hang up our wet outer clothing. "Seeing as the holiday lets are empty, I don't see any reason we shouldn't make use of one of them. We could get the fire going. The kids can watch TV. I'll bring some of the food through, and we can get really cosy. Hole up for as long as we need to."

If we are very honest, I think we both know that the chances of us returning to town today are increasingly slim.

"That's a great idea," I say. "Let's do it. In fact, let's have the big one, shall we? We should keep the Barretts' empty, just in case they do manage to get here."

"I hope they're OK," says Julie. "Isn't she pregnant, too?"

"Yes. Maybe they didn't set off. Or perhaps they're having to seek shelter in a stable."

It's no joking matter, though. I am so glad I'm not stuck out in the snow somewhere.

155

With the television and the Christmas tree lights on, I start to build a fire, while Julie gets to work in the kitchen. It is beginning to feel a bit like Christmas, even though it is not the one that any of us had planned.

Once the flames have caught, I text Sam. I feel bad for being grumpy with him earlier.

I hope you're OK xx We've been having fun in the snow, and we're all fine. I guess if we can't have the Christmas we planned, at least we're all safe and sound, with people that we love xxx

His reply message comes almost instantly. **But I wish I was with you, and Ben xxx**

I do, too. Keep an eye on the weather. You never know, it might clear xxx

I hope so xxx

'It might clear' becomes a familiar refrain in the next few hours, when I talk to Mum and Dad, and then David, who has called from the States. "I can't believe I'm missing the only white Christmas Cornwall's had in my lifetime!" he wails.

I hear Bea's voice in the background. "Well, yes, but that was barely any snow, and it doesn't count. Anyway, don't ruin my dramatic moment, Bea."

I laugh. "Ben and Zinnie are enjoying it."

"Don't rub it in, Griffiths!"

"Sorry," I laugh. "So, what's it like where you are?"

"Raining," he says ruefully. "But it's forecast to be clear tomorrow, and we're taking a trip into the mountains."

"Well, that doesn't sound too bad. And anyway, it's not that good here, because we're now all stuck apart from each other. Sam's in Devon, and I don't think he's going to be back tonight. There's no chance, really. Mum and Dad are on their own at the Sail Loft, with all the presents, and dinner for eight. Luke's with Jim, at least, and Karen is with Ron."

"So nobody's on their own?"

"No."

"And you've all got food, and drink, and roofs over your heads, and people that you love around you?"

"Yes," I concede.

"Then you'll be OK, Alice. The kids are too young to care about the presents, and you've got no choice but to sit and rest. Which it sounds like you could do with."

"You're right."

"Happy Christmas, Alice."

I feel a little sob catch in my throat at the warmth of his voice, travelling from all the way across the Atlantic.

"Happy Christmas, David. I love you."

"I love you, too."

I hear the others shouting Christmas greetings in the background.

"Send my love to everyone," I say, keenly feeling the absence of all these people – not just Sam and Mum and Dad, but all of these wonderful people who have come to be like family to me. If I had one Christmas wish, it would be to have all of them magicked here, right now, for a great big Christmas at Amethi. We really would make some memories then.

"I will. Now, go and have a good time."

I feel better for speaking to David, and I think it's time to just accept that Christmas is going to be different this year.

Meg lies in front of the fire in the lounge, while Julie serves up a spicy carrot and coriander soup, with thick slices of bread, extra mature cheddar, which crumbles in my mouth, and pickled onions so strong they make my eyes water. The baby kicks in response to all these different flavours, and I feel the warmth of the soup course through me, finally warming the tips of my fingers and toes, which have remained stubbornly red and cold since we came indoors.

"Is Luke OK?" I ask.

"He's fine," she says. "Disappointed. He was talking about walking up here, saying it's only a few miles. That's as may be on a clear day. Today, I think it would be a mistake. And Jim's not feeling great, so it's better if Luke stays with him, really. We're all just going to have a delayed Christmas."

"To be honest, this is really quite nice," I venture. "I mean, we're getting to experience what all our guests do. It'll make a great piece for the blog, as well."

"I had a message from Shona, saying we should be documenting it all on Instagram!"

"Me too. I don't think I can be bothered, though, can you?"

"No. I think that would be missing the moment, and I'm not about to post pics of Ben and Zinnie, either."

"No," I agree. "Let's just enjoy this for what it is."

"Which is me, with my amazing daughter, my best friend and her amazing son, and their lovely dog. Staying in one of Cornwall's finest self-catering cottages, amid wonderful snow-covered surroundings." She starts to sound like a holiday brochure.

"Enjoy a quiet Christmas with a top chef, in the luxurious setting of Amethi," I suggest in a breathy voice.

"Sink into the plush seating of the living room while a roaring fire crackles in the hearth."

"Can it be roaring and crackling at the same time?"

"I don't see why not."

"Take a walk in the winter wonderland of the woods, keeping an eye out for the local wildlife. Squirrels will scamper up the nearest tree at the sound of your boots trudging through the snow, while badgers hide in their snug setts, warm and cosy underground."

"Enjoy the ugly jackdaws screeching away from their treetop nests."

"They're not ugly!" I protest. "And they don't screech."

"Hmm."

"I think you've ruined the moment, Julie."

"Sorry."

After lunch, we clear up and then play some games with the children.

"This holiday cottage has been so thoughtfully stocked, with games, and DVDs," comments Julie.

"Not to mention the premier streaming services on every TV."

"But it's Christmas Eve, and Channel 4's got the classics on soon. *Father Christmas*, then *The Snowman*, then *The Snowman and the Snow Dog*."

"Perfect," I say. I am feeling a lot more relaxed than I was earlier, now that I've just given in and accepted the situation. There's nothing we can do to change it, so we might as well make the most of it.

I notice that it is almost dark outside, already. "I'll just take Meg out for a few minutes, then we'll be back."

"Shall I do some crumpets, and cheese on toast, when you're back?"

"That sounds lovely."

"And we've got mince pies," she reminds me. "I froze half of them, and got them out yesterday to defrost."

"I just wish I could have a nice glass of red wine, too."

"Maybe a little one? I don't suppose one little drop would hurt."

"We'll see."

I have to get my outdoor things from the Mowhay, and am glad to find they've dried out.

"Come on, girl," I say to Meg, who is sniffing around just outside, occasionally plunging her whole face into the snow and then pulling it back out, sneezing. She gladly comes to my side. It has at least stopped snowing now, and the thick covering on the ground adds a brightness to the otherwise dark early evening. I hear an owl call once, and then again, from the direction of the woods. Feeling brave with Meg by my side, I head that way. I've got peanuts in my pocket, to spread around for the badgers, as long as Meg is distracted elsewhere. I'm half-hoping to see the owl again, too. I was too dazed to really appreciate it when it swooped across my head that day.

As I near the woods, I stop walking, just for a moment. It is completely quiet. There is absolute stillness, and I stand like I've been frozen, not wanting to make any sound. This is a rare thing indeed and I relish the silence.

The woods are dark against an already dark sky, and I start to doubt whether I really want to go too close. Ridiculous, I know. There will not be somebody lying in wait in them, on the off-chance that a young(ish) pregnant woman might just pass by. But maybe it's not fear of anything in this world that is putting me on edge.

What with the day's events, I haven't had much of a

chance to think about what happened with the tree lights this morning. And now, with the hours that have since passed, I am not sure that I didn't imagine it. I mean, really, it's impossible. And a bit weird that it seems to be happening at Amethi as well as at home. I wonder if instead I've been having a weird hormonal optical thing. Not a migraine as such, but there must be something going on.

Never mind, I think, slipping my hand between the layers of my coat to find the warm solidity of my belly and getting moving again. I address my baby: *You'll be here soon, and I can stop being weird.* I tread firmly through the snow, feeling my feet sink, and then crunch, with each step. Meg stays right behind me, using my footprints to move more easily.

The owl calls again, and I stop. I look to the sky, but all is dark. No cloud is willing to relent and allow a glimpse of the moon or stars. Turning back, I feel proud at the sight of this beautiful place that Julie and I have helped to create here. Even though most of the rooms are empty, it looks warm, and welcoming. I reach for my phone to take another picture, then hear a rustling from the woods behind me. Meg is instantly alert, her hackles up, standing as tall as her long, lean legs will let her. My skin prickles. I turn, to see a fox, standing still and as shocked as we are, and staring straight at us.

"Leave, Meg," I say gently, carefully reaching for her collar. Then, "You can go now," I say to the fox, and it stays looking for just one more moment before it is on its way, leaping and bouncing through the snow, its brush tail straight out behind it.

Meg strains at her collar, but I'm not really sure she'd know what to do if I let her go. "Shhh," I say. "Shhh, Meg." As the fox disappears back between the trees, she relaxes, but I hold onto her for a little while longer as we start to make our way back to the house. I realise I'm shaking a little, from the shock, and it just goes to show that I'm still living on my nerves a bit. It also goes to show that I'm being ridiculous. I feel honoured to have seen the fox and, as the fear I'd felt slips away, it is replaced by elation. As we near the Mowhay, however, Meg's ears prick again, and I stop in my tracks.

I can hear what Meg's heard. Footsteps.

She takes creeping, tentative steps towards the noise. I don't know what to do. My heart is thudding. I quietly call her to me, and start to move more quickly towards the houses. But Meg doesn't come. What should I do?

Then Meg is running, leaping through the snow in her haste.

In the dark silence, I want to call for Julie, but I don't want to scare the kids, or alert anyone to my presence.

Elizabeth.

The name springs to mind as Meg begins barking, and I am frozen to the spot, with no idea what to do.

By the side of the far building, I think I can make out a shape. Yes, I'm sure there's a figure over there, near the car park. *The Barretts?* I think, my brain plucking for the rational explanation that Sam would encourage me to find, but there is no way they could have made it here.

I do move now, towards the safety of the buildings, and try to shrink into the shadows of the Mowhay. I don't want to leave Meg, but I don't know what else to do.

"Hello, Meg! Hello, girl!" I hear.

"Lizzie!" Her name bursts from my mouth with a bubble of relieved laughter. "You nearly gave me a heart attack!"

"Hello, Alice!" she calls. "Sorry, I didn't see you there. Mind if I come in? I'm freezing."

17

"You OK, Alice?" Julie calls when I step through the door. "We thought you'd got lost!"

"I'm fine," I call back, still recovering myself. "And I've got a surprise for you!"

Julie appears at the doorway. "Lizzie!" she looks almost as shocked as I feel. "What are you doing here? And how the hell did you get here?"

"That's just what I said. Come on, Lizzie. Come in from the cold, we've got a fire going. The kids will be so pleased to see you, too! Don't worry about your boots, just get into the warm."

"So you walked all the way from home?" Julie asks in disbelief, once Lizzie is settled on the seat by the fire. Ben and Zinnia are on cushions in front of the TV, watching *Father Christmas*, and sharing a bowl of crisps.

"Well, no, not quite. I drove down to the beach this morning, before the weather set in." I remember what she said, about wanting to go and see if she could find Elizabeth. I want to ask if she did, but, love Julie as I do, I know she'll find it all a bit far-fetched, so I keep quiet. "Then I tried to drive up here," Lizzie continues, "to bring your presents, and wish you both a merry Christmas, but I got stuck somewhere up on the moors. Near those standing stones, Alice."

"That's miles away!"

"Actually, as the crow flies, it's not so bad."

"So you've walked that way to get here? How on earth

did you find it? I'd be lost by now if I'd tried to do that."

"Ah, well, I've lived here all my life, haven't I?"

"Well bloody hell, Lizzie. I suppose it's better you did that than stayed in your car overnight, you'd freeze. Where are our presents, though?" Julie asks cheekily.

"I'm afraid I had to leave them in the car."

"Can you go back and get them?" I suggest, grinning.

"Yeah, sure," Lizzie grins back.

"Your clothes are still wet, Lizzie," I say. "Look, if you head over to my old place – you know, the little cottage - there are loads of things over there, which will eventually be going to charity. Some of them are Mum's, and some of them are mine. They might not be your usual taste, but at least they'll be dry, and I'm sure there's a couple of jumpers in amongst them."

"I'll do that," says Lizzie. "Thank you, Alice."

When she comes back, she's dressed in some of Mum's cords, and a pink fleece. She's also got her hair tied back. She looks like a completely different person – so much so, I almost do a double-take.

Julie goes into the kitchen and comes back with a mug of tea, and a packet of biscuits, for Lizzie. "I found your favourites! Garibaldi. Though I'll never understand what you see in them. Now, get some of these into you, woman. You must be starving. I'm about to make some cheese on toast as well. And you can have one of the rooms upstairs! I mean, I'm assuming you're not going to try and walk back again. Are you?" she asks doubtfully. Nothing would surprise us when it comes to Lizzie.

"No, I'm not!" Lizzie laughs. "And that's really kind of you. I was wondering, though, if I might stay in your old place, Alice, if you don't mind? It's so peaceful there. And I'm a bit of a solitary sort, you know, and a night owl. I don't want to keep you guys awake. Especially if Father Christmas is coming," she says, smiling towards Ben and Zinnia.

More like, she doesn't want to be woken up at 4am by the cries of 'Has he been yet?' And who can blame her?

"Of course, that's fine. Let's make sure the heating's on, and you've got firewood, and all you need. All the spare linen's over there, so it will be easy enough to make up a bed for you. Then maybe you can join us for breakfast in the morning?"

"I'd love to. I'll sort it all out, though, Alice, no need for you to worry."

"As for Father Christmas coming, we haven't got any of the kids' presents!" I say quietly.

"Oh, yes, I see what you mean. Maybe he's been delayed by snow?" Lizzie suggests.

"He's Santa!" Julie whispers. "If there's one person who shouldn't be put off by a little snow, it's him. He's got flying reindeer, for one thing."

"Good point," Lizzie says.

"I think we should just play it down. Maybe don't mention him again, and hope they kind of forget. After all, they're still pretty little."

"Father Christmas!" Ben exclaims, when we're all settled, eating cheese on toast and watching *The Snowman*.

"Santa! Santa!" shouts Zinnia.

"Presents!" shouts Ben. *Damn.* "We have to put stockings out, for presents," he explains to Lizzie. "I'm leaving mine in Mummy and Daddy's room. When are we going home?" he turns to me.

"We're going to have to stay here tonight, I think, Ben," I explain. Amid all the panicking and planning, I'd forgotten to tell him what's going on.

His face falls, then screws up. "I want Daddy."

"I know, Ben. But Daddy's with Sophie. At Jacob's house. You remember Jacob? They can't get here because of the snow."

"But I want Daddy!" he shouts.

"I know, I know," I cuddle him in to me. "As soon as the snow melts, he'll be on his way."

"When will the snow melt?"

"Soon, I hope."

"Listen, Ben," Lizzie says, "we're having a Christmas adventure, aren't we? Like in a book, or on TV. You know like the little boy there, with the Snowman? Not everybody gets to have a Christmas adventure, so we're really lucky, aren't we?"

He turns to her, looking doubtful.

"So why don't you and Mummy get some cookies for Santa, or a mince pie? And a carrot for Rudolph, and maybe you'll put your stocking out down here—"

"His stocking's at home," I mouth at her.

"—or, if you don't have your stocking here," she says, "we can use something else, can't we, Mummy? Like a pillowcase?"

I hate to see Ben's face when he comes downstairs to find an empty pillowcase in the morning, but I can't very well contradict Lizzie.

"Of course," I soothe Ben, kissing the top of his head, my mind whirring through anything we have at Amethi which might make some kind of Christmas present. At Mum and Dad's, we have a balance bike for him, plus loads of little things I've picked up over the past few months. Probably far too much, really, but I hadn't noticed it mounting up, until I'd brought it all out to wrap.

166

Sam had laughed at me. "Shall we save some for his birthday?"

"Maybe," I'd said, but wrapped it all anyway. I'd been really looking forward to putting it under the tree, and seeing Ben's face on Christmas morning.

I look at Julie and she shrugs. "I'll get some pillowcases," I say.

"And I'll go and see what we've got for Santa," says Julie.

We come back in time to watch *The Snowman and the Snowdog*. I glance at Julie at the part where the old dog dies. Both of us have tears in our eyes, then again when the new puppy appears at the end. Luckily, the death goes over Ben's and Zinnia's heads.

Lizzie watches, rapt. "I haven't seen this one before," she says. Her eyes are definitely glistening, too.

As the music fades, I stand up. "Come on then, children, let's get you upstairs for a bath, then we can put out the things for Santa, and then story time, and off to bed."

They come willingly, and I fill the bath with bubbles, recreating Ben's Father Christmas beard to make him and Zinnia laugh. I get Ben's spare clothes from my bag, hoping to find something he can wear in bed. I've learned from experience that if I don't carry spare clothes for him, it's almost guaranteed that he will spill food and drink down himself, or fall in a puddle, or roll in some mud, or all three of these things. However, it would appear that I haven't updated this change of clothes for a while, and his vest is a bit of a squeeze, while his jogging trousers are now half-masts.

I'll go over to the cottage with Lizzie after the kids are asleep, and see what I can find in amongst the hand-me-downs, so he's got something to wear tomorrow. Hopefully it's not all shorts and t-shirts. I think wistfully of the

Christmas pyjamas I'd bought for him, which are sitting in a gift bag under Mum and Dad's tree. And his Christmas jumper, folded and placed on his bed, as I'd been planning for him to put it on before we went across to the Sail Loft.

We sit the children on the seats closest to the fire, and Lizzie reads them Ben's book, *Christmas at the North Pole*. It's a *Ben and Holly* book (of course), but she changes Holly's name to Zinnia, and it makes both children giggle every time.

Julie and I smile at each other, and tiptoe into the kitchen.

"A pillowcase!" I whisper. "What are we going to fill that with?"

"I've been thinking about this," Julie says. "We've got chocolate mints, and some nice biscuits, and of course some fruit."

"Satsumas…" I say. "Classic. And I was thinking we've got the little bubble baths, soaps and shampoos."

"Excellent. Now we've filled about a fiftieth of the space. What else?"

"Their coats? We can wash them and wrap them in baking paper." I start to laugh nervously.

"I tell you what would do the job perfectly," says Julie.

"What?"

"Pillows."

I whack her on the arm. "I thought you'd actually come up with something useful!"

"We're just going to have to wing it, Alice. Once they're in bed, let's see what we've got in terms of books and DVDs in the other holiday houses. There's some playing cards, and games, too. We'll work it out. And actually, baking paper for wrapping's not a bad idea! We can always do some Blue Peter-style DIY decorating, brighten it up a bit."

"OK, OK, we can do this," I say.

We return to the lounge for the end of the story. "Time for bed, kids," I say. "Just after we've put out Santa's snacks."

They come willingly, Zinnia yawning in Julie's arms while Ben carefully arranges the two cookies and one carrot on the plate.

"Come on then, you," I say. "Say night night to Lizzie."

Ben runs to her and gives her a huge hug. She looks surprised and delighted. "Night, night, young'un," she says.

Upstairs, we use some of the spare toothbrushes and toothpaste we keep for guests, and I tuck Ben into the double bed. "I'll just be downstairs," I say, "with Auntie Julie, then I'll sleep in here with you tonight. Is that OK?"

"Yes, Mummy," he yawns.

"No snoring, though," I say firmly.

This makes him giggle. "You snore, Mummy."

"I do not." I pretend to be shocked by this accusation. "I'll stay here with you while you go to sleep, shall I?"

"Yes, please."

I watch his face, while he lets sleep take over. His delicate eyelids, tiny blue veins threaded across them, flutter a little while he puts up some gentle resistance, and then he is breathing steady and deeply. I stay for just a few more moments and then, keeping the bedside light on, I leave the room.

"It's snowing again," Julie says, when I get downstairs.

"Oh no."

"Oh yes."

"It's getting windy, too," says Lizzie.

This is not what I wanted to hear, but I see Lizzie watching my face and the word *breathe* springs to mind, so I do. I inhale long and slow, and exhale longer and slower.

"I'll head off to the cottage now, if you don't mind. You two must be tired," she says.

"I am, actually," I say, rubbing my eyes. "I hadn't realised quite how much, till now."

"You must be exhausted too, Lizzie, after your huge walk through the snow."

"I'm fine! I'll sleep when I need to."

I walk across to the cottage with her, and when we get there, Meg wants to go in.

"No, Meg," I say, "we're not staying here tonight."

"I don't mind," says Lizzie. "I'll appreciate her company."

"Are you sure?"

"Of course. I can let her out a bit later, and you can go to bed as soon as you need to."

I look at my watch. "It's only 8pm!"

"Doesn't matter," Lizzie says. "You get that sleep when you can. You never know when you'll need extra energy."

I yawn, and stoop to stroke Meg, who is standing inside the cottage doorway. "Are you staying here tonight, Meg? Don't go changing your mind, will you?"

"She'll be fine," Lizzie says. "I'll get the fire going, and she can sit up with me."

"Have you got a book or something? There are some in amongst all that other stuff. Just have a rummage through, and help yourself to anything, won't you? And there's tea and coffee, and loads of stuff over in the main kitchen. Sorry, I should have thought to get you some…"

Lizzie puts her hand on my arm and smiles. "Alice, it's all OK! I know where everything is, and I'll sort myself out. I'm just grateful to you and Julie for being so hospitable."

"Alright, if you're sure." I hug her. "Happy Christmas, Lizzie. Or I suppose I should say Merry Yuletide. Or is it too late for that?"

"Either is fine!" she smiles and says firmly, "Goodnight, Alice."

"Goodnight, Lizzie." I take her not very subtle hint and turn away, walking back through the snow, which glistens in the lights from the houses. I think of Ben and Zinnia, asleep in those big beds. Then my mind goes to Sam, and Sophie. I hope they're OK. I am sure they will be. But it's strange to think I won't have Christmas morning with Sam.

I am tearful, all of a sudden, and I stand in the cold and let the tears come, wiping them clear of my face and drying my eyes before I go in to find my best friend, and plonk myself next to her, leaning my head on her shoulder.

"Alright, Griffiths?" She tips her head to rest on mine.

"Yeah. I think so."

"At least it will be memorable," she says.

"True!" I laugh. Then I start to cry again.

"Come on, it'll be OK. It's OK. And Ben got his Christmas snow, didn't he? So he's happy."

"True." I pull a tissue from my pocket, sit up and blow my nose.

"Urgh. You foul creature!" Julie says, making me laugh.

"Thank you, Julie," I say.

"For what?"

"For making today fun. If it had been down to me, it would have been miserable and depressing."

"Well, that's the difference between me and you, isn't it? It's why people always like me, but can't stand you."

I laugh again. "Thanks very much."

"Got to face the facts sometime, Alice."

After checking that the children are definitely asleep, under cover of darkness, we sneak across to the main kitchen, and raid it for as many treats as we can find. Then to the store cupboard, for toiletries and stationery. There are lots of things, once we start to get creative. We pile a load of them into boxes, and carry them back across to the house. By the light of the fire, we put string and pasta tubes into sandwich bags, to make do-it-yourself necklace kits. We wrap toiletries in flannels, and tie them with string. Plastic tubs are filled halfway with rice, to make percussion instruments. We top up the rice with glitter, which for some reason Julie has in her handbag. "It's from a party bag. It fell out, and I decided to keep it. How did I know it would come in handy one day?"

"You genius!" I say, kissing her and finding my own huge bag. Alongside ill-fitting clothes, it contains quite an array of items I've gathered over time: puzzle books and small packets of coloured pencils they give out at pubs to help keep kids entertained while they wait for their food; Kinder chocolate bars; tiny bottles of bubbles. Even a couple of those little rubber monster finger puppets.

Then Julie has a brainwave. "I'll just get some jars," she says. "I'll be right back." She mixes food colouring, salt and oil in the jars, then tips in some glitter and tops it all up with water, fixing the lids on firmly with glue. She produces a torch from her pocket, shakes one of the jars, then turns on the torch. Coloured globules float around in the jar. "A home-made lava lamp!" she says. "We made them once at the Eden Project! My god, when did I get so bloody mumsy?"

When we've run out of ideas, and wrapped the gifts as best we can, we put them carefully in the pillowcases, but there is still a lot of empty space.

"I'm starting to think your pillow idea's not so bad after all," I say.

"It'll be fine, Alice. Little kids don't care. They're too

172

young to have expectations, it'll just seem so magical to them, that somebody's been and left them these gifts. Good job they're not any older, though, I don't think we'd get away with this then! Now, let's have another drink before we go to bed."

Julie gets herself a miniature whisky, while I have a hot chocolate. We turn the lights off, apart from those on the Christmas tree, which I am relieved to see stay on, and sit in the glow of the fire.

"Merry Christmas, Julie," I say, clinking my mug against her glass.

"Merry Christmas, Alice."

We sit quietly for a while, each happy with our own thoughts, then head on upstairs, hugging on the landing before we go in to our children. Ben is breathing quietly when I tiptoe into my room and I slide into bed as quietly as I can, and lie for a while, just listening to him. Then I pick up my phone and message Sam, then Mum and Dad. Checking in on them all, and wanting some kind of contact. I feel a long way from everyone, snowed in up here, and all the more so for this being Christmas Eve. It's been busy enough to lose myself in the moment today, but now I'm alone again, I feel strongly how much I am missing. Tears wet my eyes, but I wipe them away. It would not do for Ben to wake and see his mum crying.

A ping, as a message comes back in.

Mum: **I'm glad you're OK, Alice, and don't worry. We miss you too, of course, but we'll celebrate properly as soon as we can. You've a lot to look forward to and you'll be back home soon xxx**

Another ping.

Dad: **Happy Christmas, Alice. It's not the same without you and Ben and Sam here, but we'll be together again very soon. And you'll have a great story to tell. Get some sleep now! xx**

Then from Sam: **Night night, my love. Don't fret, Soph and I will be back with you as soon as we possibly can. They say it should start to melt tomorrow, and they're clearing the main roads - poor buggers, it's their Christmas too! Give Ben a kiss from me, and have one for you too. I love you. Xxx**

I love you too xxx

I feel better just for hearing from them, and I close my eyes, let exhaustion claim me. At some time in the night, I think I hear something. *Father Christmas*, I think sleepily, smiling to myself. I crack my eyes open enough to see Ben right there next to me, and know that all is well, then I fall back into a deep sleep, and don't wake until morning.

18

I wake to the sound of Julie's voice somewhere close to my head. "Alice! Wake up!"

Why is she whispering? Why is she in my room?

I notice the light is different. Brighter. Whiter. Then it hits me, where we are. Why we're here. What day it is!

Ben, I think, and I turn, to see him still slumbering away, arms flung above his head and duvet pushed off, totally chilled, and as though nothing out of the ordinary has happened.

"Alice!" Zinnia, held securely on Julie's hip, laughs loudly and suddenly, and yet Ben still does not stir.

"What time is it?" I ask, quietly.

"Nearly eight."

"Eight? On Christmas Day?"

"I know! Unheard of! I don't think you'll be getting away with any Christmas lie-ins again. Not for a few years yet, anyway."

"Has he been?" I grin.

"Well, actually," Julie says, mysteriously, "Yes."

"What?" I sit up suddenly, which does disturb Ben. My first thought is Sam, but that doesn't really make any sense. If he was here, he'd have been up to find us.

"I went down to put some coffee on, while this one was still sleeping," she jiggles Zinnia, making her giggle, "and, well... You'd better come and see for yourself."

"Is it Christmas?" Ben asks.

"Yes! It is, Ben. Happy Christmas," I swoop in on him and kiss him, then blow raspberries all over his face.

"Get off!" he giggles.

"Auntie Julie says Father Christmas has been." I look at her questioningly, and she nods. "Shall we go and see?"

"Yes!" Suddenly, he is scrambling out of bed.

"Wait for me, Ben," I say. "Let's all go together."

The first surprise is the hallway. Mingled in with those mistletoe garlands that adorn the banisters are twinkling fairy lights, which I know for a fact were not there when we went to bed last night. Neither were the holly boughs behind the mirror, or the mistletoe hanging behind the front door.

"That's nothing," Julie says, and she opens the door to the lounge.

I gasp. All the windowsills are adorned with more holly, tealights and lanterns – which I recognise from the yoga workshops. *Lizzie*, I smile to myself. The dining table has a holly wreath in its centre, surrounding a large, white, real candle, the flame flickering slightly as we enter the room. A fire is merrily dancing away in the hearth, and in front of it those pillow cases, which had looked so paltry and pathetic last night, sit stuffed full. I look at Julie again, and she shrugs.

"Didn't you take a peek?" I asked.

"No! I didn't want to ruin the magic."

The children don't take long to notice. "Look, Zinnie," says Ben, and takes her hand as they walk slightly nervously towards them. I remember Ben's discomfort at the thought of a strange man entering the house – even if it is a strange man with presents.

"It's OK, Benny," I say, hoping I'm right. After all, I have no idea what lies within. But of course, Lizzie being Lizzie, it is more than alright.

The first item Ben pulls from the sack is a large stuffed replica of the Snowman. "Look, Mummy!"

"Oh wow," I say. "Look at that!"

Zinnia, meanwhile, has taken what looks like a toy Snowdog from her sack. "Doggy!" she shouts excitedly.

Julie looks at me, and I know my smile is as wide as hers. How the hell has Lizzie managed this? Don't tell me she walked back to her car. No, she can't possibly have done.

The children can't wait to pull out their other gifts, and amongst the items we prepared last night come also toy dinosaurs on wheels, model cars, card games, and books. None brand new, by the looks of things, but that doesn't bother the kids one bit. Julie and I sit on the settee behind them, watching in awe.

"If I haven't said it before, I bloody love Lizzie," Julie says, quietly.

"I know. She's gone above and beyond here. But how?"

Julie retrieves the discarded Snowman from behind Ben and hands it to me. "Home-made," she whispers. "Look."

I examine it, turning it over and realising it's been made from a t-shirt turned inside out so the logo can only be seen if you press on the material. It's one of Sam's old ones.

"She made this last night!" I say as quietly as I possibly can.

"She can't have!"

"She bloody can."

"But she can't have… she can't have done all this. Has she made the Snowdog, too?"

Julie tries to take the dog from Zinnia, but there is no way the little girl is letting go now she has a dog of her own.

"I guess so."

"My god."

"I know."

It takes only about half an hour or so for the presents to all be revealed, and then the children don't know what to play with first.

"Tell you what," says Julie, "shall we have some breakfast? I can make pancakes!"

"Yes!" Ben says.

"I'll just see if Lizzie's up, shall I? Invite her over."

"Of course! Yes, of course. Get her over here right now!"

I pull on my coat, and step outside, into an Amethi I have never seen before. I remember we got Christmas cards made up of this place covered in snow one year. This looks just like them, only a hundred times better. The lights are still on across all the houses, and there's a breeze on the air, swaying them ever so gently, and making them sparkle like stars. The Christmas tree, too, is brought alive, and I stop for just a moment to look at it. Overhead, a pair of crows fly; strong beaks pointed firmly forwards. I rub at the snow on one of the bird tables, seeing if there is any food underneath. I'll sort out the feeders in a little while. The birds will need their Christmas breakfast, too.

Over at the cottage, the curtains are closed, and all is quiet. I suspect Lizzie has been up all night. She must have been. So I won't disturb her. But I do open the door quietly, to be greeted by a joyful Meg.

"Come on," I whisper. "Let's get you some breakfast, shall we?"

Then, hit by a sudden flash of inspiration, I write 'THANK YOU LIZZIE' in large letters in the snow below the bedroom windows, hoping she will see it when she wakes and opens the curtains. Also hoping that it is not going to snow anymore and cover up the letters, or, more importantly, prevent Sam from getting here. A white Christmas is all very well, but we have had snow enough, thanks very much.

"I think she's still asleep," I say, when I get back into the house, Meg rushing in to greet everybody. I close the door

178

swiftly, to be enveloped by the warmth from the radiators and the fire.

"She must have worked through the night," says Julie. "I'm just putting on the TV for these two, then I'll get the pancakes going."

I am very hungry, I realise. "Remember I'm eating for two, won't you?"

"Of course! Now you go and sit down. I'm doing this."

"Shall I at least set the table...?"

"I said sit down, Alice!" she laughs.

"Alright, alright! I'm going."

Julie makes a stack of pancakes, and prepares a fruit salad of tangerine slices, tinned peaches, and mango, grapes and apple. There is a metal jug of hot chocolate, a glass jug of orange juice, a small mug of lemon juice, and jars of brown sugar, maple syrup, and honey. She has also brought out a jar of granola and some natural yoghurt.

"Wow," I say. "This looks amazing."

"It is. Because I did it."

"And you're so modest," I tell her.

"Yes, everybody tells me that, after they've told me how brilliant I am, and I can't help but agree."

The children kneel on the chairs so they can reach the table, and we help them cover their pancakes in lemon juice and honey, then we help ourselves.

"These are so good," I say, already on my second pancake, wiping a sticky drip of maple sauce from my chin. "Thank you, Julie. And Merry Christmas, all of you."

We raise our glasses, and the kids their plastic cups.

Julie looks around at us all, and smiles. "To the best Christmas we can possibly have, and to a happy new year."

19

By about half ten, however, we are already starting to feel fatigued. I am really tired, and I am missing Sam, and Sophie. And Mum and Dad. I have spoken to them all, and we've wished each other unconvincingly cheery Merry Christmases. This is not the Christmas that any of us had been looking forward to. At least we are all safe and well, though. I have also heard from the Barretts, who did indeed get stuck on their journey down, and have been put up at an inn near Bodmin.

I feel a bit like we're Mary and Joseph, the email read. **But I really, really hope I'm not going to give birth in a stable. We're hopeful that the snow is going to clear in the next day or so, and are still intending to come down, though we're very sorry not to have been there for Christmas Day. And apologies again for not letting you know where we were, but there was a power cut here, and we could not get any mobile signal, WiFi, nothing. It was a candle-lit Christmas Eve in the bar, and felt quite jolly really, but we're looking forward to arriving at Amethi, and are saving our presents to open there.**

It's a relief that they are alright, and I smile at the Mary and Joseph reference, though I bet they'd get a load of free nappies and babywear if they had their own real-life nativity story to tell.

But I'm running out of steam, and fast. A quick blood pressure test shows it's a little high again, and I think I'm feeling it. What would happen, if I got ill now? Or went into labour? It doesn't bear thinking about. I need to keep my thoughts positive. Lizzie and Julie have been making so much effort, but I just want to be at home, or at the Sail Loft. But this is not possible, I know, and I need to keep a cheerful face on things.

I see Julie is looking a little glum herself. She's messaging Luke.

"Bet he's missing you and Zinnie," I say.

"Yeah. I don't think he's having a lot of fun. Jim is poorly, still, and it's just the two of them."

"That's not great. Poor blokes. Maybe we should have a walk to the car in a while – see how the roads are looking. It might be good for the kids to get a bit of exercise and fresh air, as well."

"Good idea, my friend," she puts her phone away and smiles at me. "No slipping over, though. I don't want any health and safety lawsuits."

"Wouldn't I be suing myself?" I say, laughing. "Anyway, I don't intend to be slipping anywhere. I will walk nice and slowly, and if it's really slippery, you can carry me back here."

"Sure, no problem."

She nips across to the Mowhay to collect the kids' coats, hats and gloves that we left to dry yesterday, while I turn off the TV and get Ben and Zinnia into their wellies.

"Snowball fight!" says Ben.

"Yes, yes, snowman. Snowdog!" Zinnia chants.

"We'll see," I say. "First off, we'll have a little walk to see if we can find the car, shall we? And see if the snow's started to melt."

They don't look massively enthused at the prospect, and I can't say I blame them.

Outside, the children are almost as excited as they were yesterday. The Secular Snow Singers are partially covered in a thin layer of more recent snow, but it's not a lot, so hopefully we are on the turn now, towards clear skies, and, more importantly, clear roads.

"I'll just see if Lizzie's up yet," Julie says, trekking across to the cottage, but she comes back shaking her head. "She must be shattered. I'll leave her till nearly lunchtime, then get her to come and eat with us. Surely she'll be hungry, and won't want to miss out on Christmas dinner."

I walk carefully with the others, very seriously not wanting to fall. I have a real fear of falling onto the bump, and the baby taking the brunt of it. Meg runs along with the children, chasing their snowballs, and making up for the lack of energy from their mums.

"I'm not feeling it now, Alice, are you?" Julie admits.

"No, not really. This morning was really lovely," I say. "Yesterday, too. But it doesn't feel the same, somehow, with everyone separated. Still, it was so absolutely amazing of Lizzie to do all that stuff."

"I know. But… don't you just want to be home?"

"Yep. At least they're happy, though," I gesture with my head towards our children, who have fallen on their backs to make snow angels.

"Yeah. I guess we just have to carry on making the most of it."

"And, you never know, maybe the roads will be more friendly by now."

They're not. The snow has piled up against the hedgerows in huge drifts. The car is more or less visible, but has been thoroughly hemmed in.

"Shit," says Julie.

"Bugger."

There is no point trying to free the car – even if we did, it won't be going anywhere for a while. We traipse back to the house, and I notice some wisps of smoke coming from Lizzie's chimney. "I'll go and see if she's coming over," I say.

"Yes, please say thanks to her from me, and tell her I'm making lunch and she has to come."

"I will."

I knock on the door and Lizzie opens it, back in her own, more familiar clothes now. "Alice!" she says. "Merry Christmas!"

"Happy Christmas," I say, hugging her. "I was wondering, did you happen to hear any sleigh bells, or hooves on your roof last night?"

"No," she says, wide-eyed. "I slept right through."

"Well, we definitely had a visit from Santa. The children were so excited, and the house looks so beautiful, too. Thank you so much, Lizzie."

"It was absolutely my pleasure, I promise. Did they like the Snowman and Snowdog?"

"They love them. We had to prise the dog out of Zinnie's hands before she went outside."

"I'm so pleased."

"You're pretty nifty, aren't you?"

"Well, I enjoy it. And I've usually got my craft kit with me. It's all in my Bag of Many Things."

"What else is in there?" I ask.

"That's for me to know, and you to find out."

"Julie's about to start making lunch, so do you want to come over when you're ready? No rush, I think it will be a good hour or so. But come over before then if you want.

Whenever you like."

"That will be lovely. Thank you, Alice. I was about to do a quick fifteen minutes' yoga, so I'll have a shower and come round after that."

Yoga on Christmas Day! Usually, I'd be on my third mince pie and second sherry by now. I don't think yoga would have crossed my mind. "Brilliant. And honestly, Lizzie, thank you so very much. You've made Christmas for us."

"You were already making it work, I just helped you on your way a little."

I'm smiling as I walk back to 'our house', and I am sure that the day seems just a little bit brighter. It doesn't feel quite so cold anymore, either. I look to the sky. "You're up there somewhere," I say to the hiding sun. "I know you are. Come on out, we need you."

"Who are you talking to, you nutter?" Julie is at the door, waiting for me, with an empty log basket.

"The sun."

"He's inside already... oh you mean the actual sun, not Ben. Lizzie's getting into your head, isn't she, you bloody hippy?"

"Maybe a little."

"Go on in, I'll just get some more wood for the fire."

"I'll put the kettle on."

"Brill."

Julie won't let me do too much to help, but she does allow me to peel and chop the potatoes.

"Cut some into wedges, too, for the kids. I'm doctoring the menu, so we'll all have breaded mozzarella, with roasties for us, and wedges for Ben and Zinnie. You could make the bruschetta to start, as well, if you don't mind."

"You trust me with them, do you?"

"Well… let's just say they've got the least potential for ruining. If you manage to burn *them*, I'll be impressed."

"Have faith, my friend. Have faith!"

As we make ourselves busy in the kitchen, taking it in turns to pop our heads round the door and check on the children, who are being watched over by Meg, I start to feel some of the Christmas cheer return.

There's a knock on the door. "Come on in, Lizzie!" I call.

"Funny she's knocking, when she was happy to let herself in during the night!" Lizzie laughs.

I hear the door pushed open. "Knock, knock." That's not Lizzie!

"Grandpa!" Ben shouts, and my jaw drops. I hurry through to see Ben throwing himself at Dad, who is followed by Mum, and Karen, and Ron.

"What the…? How…?"

"We got a lift!" Dad says. "On a snow plough!"

"You did what?"

"Merry Christmas, Alice!" He hugs and kisses me, his skin cold against mine.

"Happy Christmas, love," Mum hugs me for just a little longer than Dad did. "I'm so glad you're OK." She presses a kiss against my ear.

"I'm fine," I laugh, fighting a sudden urge to cry. "And so glad to see you."

"It's all thanks to this gentleman," Dad says, gesturing to Ron, while I hug Karen, and then Ron himself. "Or his friend, to be more precise."

"Well, Karen wouldn't stop going on about how much she was missing you all, and how she wanted to see Ben, and I called in a favour."

"Some favour!" Julie says. "I don't suppose you

happened to see my car on the way past?"

"Oh, was that yours, Julie? Bill's managed to clear a lot of the snow, so it's not so deep now. Still icy, mind," Ron says.

"We were just getting dinner ready," Julie says. "If I'd have known we were having company, I'd have prepared the fish."

"No need to worry about that!" Mum laughs. "It was a toss-up between bringing presents and bringing food and drink, and I'm afraid food and drink won the battle." In the hallway there are numerous insulated bags. "We hatched this plan this morning, just after talking to you, Alice, and while Ron was sorting out our lift, we all got cooking."

"There's roast spuds, gravy, turkey – sorry, Alice, but you know it's not Christmas to me without turkey." Dad takes over. "And pigs in blankets, too. But we've got roast parsnips, and nut loaf, and Yorkshire puds."

"Wow!"

"I did the puddings," Karen says. "We've got cherry pie, and chocolate cake for my little prince! You love Granny's chocolate cake, don't you?" She sweeps Ben up for a cuddle, kissing him until he protests.

"We may have brought some wine as well," says Dad. "We thought if the snow's melted by this evening, we could get a taxi home."

"Or call Bill and his plough again!" Ron laughs.

"I'm just sorry we couldn't bring any presents," Mum says, conspiratorially. "I don't suppose Santa's been able to put in an appearance?"

"Actually, Mum, Father Christmas knew we were here, and he left lots of lovely things, didn't he, kids?"

"Yes! Yes!" Ben and Zinnia are energised by this new

turn in the day, and an influx of visitors who want nothing more than to admire their new presents and hear all about the snowball fights, and snowman-building.

When Lizzie appears, she is shocked and pleased at the attention she's given.

"I hear you saved Christmas," Dad says.

"I wouldn't say that," she responds modestly.

"No, but I would. All of these lovely lights, the mistletoe, the holly," I say, gesturing around the room, "is all thanks to Lizzie."

Looking at the table, I realise there is no way we can all fit around it, or that all the food can fit onto it. "I think we'd better eat in the Mowhay," I say. "Maybe if I head over there with Lizzie, you guys can keep the kids entertained, or help Julie in the kitchen." I hope that's OK with Julie, and I want to get Lizzie somewhere a bit less overwhelming.

We walk companionably and Lizzie says, "Stop."

"What?"

I follow the direction of her gaze and see what she's noticed. The sun is pushing its way through the clouds. Slowly, but definitely. I hear a drip behind me.

"It's melting!" I say, jubilantly. "The snow is melting!"

"We've a way to go yet!" laughs Lizzie.

The Mowhay is as quiet as a church. Our footsteps echo across the floor, and it reminds me of last night. Hearing Lizzie, and just for a moment thinking she was a ghost. I shake my head, laughing inwardly at myself. I still haven't worked out what was going on with the Christmas tree lights, but it hasn't happened again, and I'm increasingly sure I must have imagined it, or it was my mind playing visual tricks on me.

187

We get the heating on, and go into the kitchen to get plates, bowls, glasses and cutlery. Lizzie fetches a wreath from one of the holiday let doors, and places it in the centre of the table. "Would it be OK to get the candle from your house?" she asks. "It's the Yuletide candle, which I lit last night. Some people think it's a sign of bad luck if it's gone out by morning, but this one kept burning."

"Ah, yes of course. I hate to say it, but we blew it out when we went out for our walk."

"That's fine!" she smiles. "I'll light it again now, though, shall I?"

"Yes! And should we get some of the little tealights and lanterns, too?"

"Perfect."

Though I feel like I am more tired than I have ever been in my life, and I wish so much that Sam and Sophie were here, the day has been given a new lease of life. Thanks to so many of the wonderful people in my life, Christmas has well and truly been saved.

20

Dinner is a very jolly affair, despite us missing a few key people. Ron's presence softens Karen, somehow, and he and Dad get on well anyway, having a very similar sense of humour. Dad keeps topping up Ron's glass.

"Phil," says Mum warningly.

"It's Christmas!" he protests.

Ben and Zinnia love being centre of attention, and Meg loves her serving of Christmas turkey. Frustratingly, with all this delicious food on hand, the baby is taking up so much space now that I start to feel uncomfortably full after only clearing about half my plate.

"Are you OK, Alice?" Mum asks.

"Oh, yeah," I smile. "Just saving room for pudding."

While Dad and Ron clear the plates away, I excuse myself, and go outside for some fresh air. There is the regular sound of dripping now, from the roofs and the gutters, and the trees. The overbearing snow clouds have left us behind, leaving an opening for the cold, thin blue of the sky.

A blackbird skitters across the snow-covered ground, twittering rapidly until it reaches the safety of the hedgerow. Behind me are the good-natured voices of my family and friends. But I want to see Sam, so much.

We're just having lunch, I message him. **Mum, Dad, your mum and Ron have all turned up. On a snow plough! I wish you were here, though. xxx**

I heard that Bill came to the rescue! he replies quickly. **But why didn't he pick you and Julie up and take you home instead? xxx**

Bloody hell. In all the excitement, I hadn't even thought that was an option! Never mind. I suppose we were already cooking, and cosy and warm in our holiday house. Still… it would have been nice to get home.

I don't know. That would actually have made more sense. Don't mention it, though. I think they were all so pleased with themselves, surprising us like they did xxx

Looks like the snow's beginning to melt now. We're hoping to leave sometime after lunch. It's just taking a while. Isaac's cooking…

I see! Well, hopefully we'll all be back home, safe and sound, by tonight.

I hope so. Miss you so much, Alice. Let's never have Christmas apart again xxx

It's a deal. I miss you, too. I'd better go back in. Pudding is calling! xxx

You're making me hungry. Hope Isaac hurries up. See you later xxx

Cheered by the thought of seeing Sam, and having him and Sophie back home, I return to the warmth of the Mowhay.

"The snow's starting to melt!" I tell everyone. There are cheers from Dad and Ron. "And Sam and Sophie are heading home after lunch!" More cheers. I smile and sit down, ready to enjoy a selection of desserts.

Annoyingly, as with the main course, I am stopped in my tracks, by the lack of space. "Blooming baby!" I say. "How can I eat for two, when there's barely enough room for one?"

"It'll be here before you know it," says Karen. "I remember Janie came much more quickly than our Sam."

"I hope so," I say. "I think I've had enough of being pregnant now."

I watch enviously, as the others enjoy their first, and second, and in one case (Dad) third, helping of pudding. Then I stand to help clear the things away, but nobody will hear of it.

"OK, OK," I give in.

While the urn heats up for coffee and tea, we eat after-dinner mints and tell each other cracker jokes. Ben laughs his head off at all of them, which makes everybody else laugh.

Then Ron is tapping his glass with a spoon. We all look at him.

"Ladies and gentlemen," he says, "I just wanted to wish each and every one of you a happy Christmas, and an even happier new year. I've been so grateful for the way you've welcomed me into your family group, and I'm not sure I've ever enjoyed Christmas more."

We all smile and murmur our appreciation, of his sentiments, and of Ron himself. But he's not finished yet.

"And I have something that I want to ask Karen," he says, almost nervously smiling at her, while her already pink cheeks flush bright red. "Karen, my love," he says. "I have not had anywhere near as much fun with anyone as I have with you. And I would be so very happy if you'd do me the honour of being my wife."

He is down on his knee, a small jewellery box fitting snugly into the palm of his hand.

"Oh Ron, oh yes, Ron. Yes, I'd love to."

Karen is in tears, and I'd say the majority of the rest of us are as well. We cheer and applaud, then I jerk suddenly upwards, pushing my seat back so that it falls to the floor.

"Alice?" Mum says, and everyone is looking at me. "Are you alright?"

"Yes, just a sharp pain," I say. "Probably indigestion. All that rich food, you know."

But Lizzie is watching me like a hawk. It seems that she knows better.

21

The pains come and go throughout the afternoon, some worse than others.

"Why don't you try and get some rest, love?" asks Mum, but I'm reluctant to go up to bed while everybody is downstairs, and I don't want to miss out on Ben's Christmas, particularly as Sam isn't here yet.

"I'll be alright, thank you, Mum. Honestly, it's probably all the rich food, and maybe a bit of stress, too. The baby's not due for another four weeks. It could even be Braxton Hicks," I say, instantly regretting it.

"Why? Does it feel like contractions?" she asks, alarmed.

"No, no. Not really. In fact, not. As far as I remember!" I try to laugh the whole thing off, but she is not buying it, and neither are Lizzie, Karen, or Julie.

"I'll go and check the roads with Ron," Dad says. "See if we can get back to town yet."

"Alright," Mum says. "Why don't you take Ben with you?"

"And Zinnia!" I say. Somehow, I don't want this to become a male vs female thing, with the women staying to look after me, while the men folk go out to check on the roads. Besides, I know Zinnia will keep Ben entertained, and they could both do with some more fresh air.

"Of course," Ron says, and I think how he is probably the most qualified person here, if I did go into labour, but the image of him helping me give birth does not sit well, somehow.

"Where's your blood pressure monitor, love?" Mum asks,

193

when the four expeditionaries have left the building, and we can hear the excited chatter of Ben and Zinnia as they throw themselves into the snow-play once more.

"It's in my room," I say.

"I'll get it," Julie springs into action, while Mum almost physically forces me to get my feet up on the settee, elevating them with a couple of cushions.

"Ow! Mum! That's actually really uncomfortable!" I protest.

"Oh, I'm sorry, love. It's been so long, I can't remember what's right and wrong."

"It's different for everyone," Lizzie interjects gently. "Alice needs to find her own comfortable position."

"I'm not in labour yet!" I insist.

Lizzie looks at me.

"I'm not!"

Actually, I am. In the next hour or two, the pains become more defined, and more regular, although they are still comfortingly far apart.

I've called Sam, who was already about to leave, but is startled into action by this new development.

"He was in the car like a shot! Nearly forgot me!" Sophie chirps over the phone when they're on their way. "Are you OK, Alice? What does it feel like?"

"I'm OK," I laugh. "And what does it feel like? It's difficult to say, really. I'm fine when I'm not having a contraction. Just pretty normal, really. But they're painful, when they come. I just have to squeeze my eyes as tightly shut as possible, and ride them out."

"They're going to get worse, as well," Karen says helpfully.

I don't reply to this. "Just tell Sam to take his time, and

don't rush to get here. The roads are still going to be a bit tricky. I'd rather you get here in one piece. I'll be fine, I promise."

I have called Sandi, the midwife, apologising for interrupting her Christmas.

"Oh, don't you worry about that, my love. I'm on call, I expect it! But you're a little bit early, aren't you, so you're right, it could be a false alarm. Just keep on timing them, and keep an eye on your blood pressure, too, alright? I'll check in with you in an hour or so, but call me in the meantime, if you need me, OK?"

"OK," I agree.

When Ron and Dad had returned, they said that the snow was definitely melting, but the roads were going to take a little while. Annoyingly, where the snow plough has been, it's compacted the snow, so it might actually take longer to clear. But still, it's positive news.

"Any other year, I'd be delighted to have a white Christmas!" I say. "In fact, I think I've dreamed of it since I was a kid. Typical, the one time it happens, it's more of an inconvenience than the magical experience I'd imagined!"

"Ah well, these things can't be helped," says Mum. "And at least Sam's on his way now, too. Where's Luke now, Julie?"

"He's still at Jim's. They're having the worst time of all of us, I think. Jim's not up to eating much, and is wiped out by this infection, and he's giving himself a hard time for letting down the people at the soup kitchen. And actually, in between looking after his dad, Luke's been doing some work."

"He hasn't!" I laugh.

"He has. He said he might as well do it now, then make

the most of being with me and Zinnie when we're back together."

"Can't fault his practicality, I suppose," I muse. "But still, it's Christmas Day."

"It's like you've said, though, Alice. If it's not a good Christmas – if you're lonely, bereaved, heartbroken, whatever – maybe it's better to almost ignore it. Pretend it's not happening, and just breathe a sigh of relief when it's over, and life returns to normal."

"It's not so awful for Luke though, is it?"

"No, but I think he and Jim are really feeling May's absence, with Marie up at her boyfriend's as well, and just the two of them in the house."

"What about your mum, Julie?" Mum asks.

"Well, she's gutted she couldn't get down here, but she's with Lee and his family now, so it's not too bad. And she said she's going to try and swing some extra days off for New Year. We're going to take her out down the town in fancy dress! She'll love it."

I grip the nearest hand to mine as a particularly bad pain comes on. "I'm starting to think this is the real deal," I say.

"I think you're right," says Lizzie.

"But what am I going to do?" I say plaintively, trying to keep calm, so as not to panic Ben – or anyone else, for that matter. "I can't very well give birth here, can I?"

"It might not come to that yet," says Mum.

"You think we should call an ambulance?"

"No," says Lizzie firmly. "There's a way to go yet, and anyway, I don't think an ambulance would have any more luck getting up here. If we ring for one, you could end up being airlifted, up to Plymouth. I don't think you want that."

"I don't want that," I confirm.

"But you can't just stay here," Mum says. "None of us are midwives. How do we know what to do? What if something–" I can see she regrets beginning this sentence – "goes wrong?"

"It will be OK, Sue," Lizzie says, and I can see this gets Mum's back up.

"It's all very well, saying that," she says, "but this is my daughter. My grandchild."

"And they're going to be alright."

"How can you possibly know that?" Mum snaps.

"It's alright, Mum. Lizzie's just trying to help, and keep us calm."

"I'm perfectly calm, thank you."

I need to intervene, and I feel suddenly, surprisingly, calm and in control. "Mum, Lizzie, Julie, Karen, there is a chance that you are about to witness, and perhaps help in, the birth of my second child today. Now, I love you all dearly, and I know that all of you only want the best for me, and the baby. This may yet come to nothing, but if it does, I need it to be positive and as relaxed as possible. You know my blood pressure's been up, so I need to make sure it doesn't get worse. I also need to make sure that when this baby arrives, it is into a happy, positive atmosphere. You can do as Ron and Dad are doing–" I glance over to them. They are studiously playing a board game with Zinnia and Ben, trying to look like they're not listening – "and keep the kids amused. Or you can be involved in this, if you like, but we all need to be working together. OK? Lecture over. Sorry."

"That's OK, love," Mum says. "And you're right. It's a stressful time for us all, though."

"I know that. I know it is. Now, the most pressing thing I need to work out is where to go."

"Go?" asks Karen. "You're not going anywhere, my love! The roads are all blocked, remember?"

"I think Alice means where to be, if she is going to give birth," says Julie.

"I've already thought of that," Lizzie says, half apologetically, looking to my mum. She doesn't want to tread on anybody's toes. "Sue, would you come with me and see if you think this is a good idea?"

Thank you, Lizzie, I think. For being on the ball, and for deliberately involving Mum. Having said that, I'd quite like to make my own mind up, but suddenly I'm seeing the bigger picture, of all of us who are here this Christmas. Two little children. A dog. Three grandparents-to-be – make that four, now it looks like Ron is going to be an official part of the family – my best friend, and our yoga instructor. That's not fair on Lizzie. She is so much more than that. Let's say another very good, close friend. Hopefully soon I can add my husband and stepdaughter to this list.

But for now, it's just the ten of us, including Meg, and Christmas belongs to us all. A much-needed break from work for Mum and Dad, though it's not quite as they'd imagined it might be. And Ron and Karen have just got engaged! They should be enjoying a bit more attention. It's the kids' first Christmas that they might just remember. And Julie is missing Luke, and her mum, while Lizzie is – well, Lizzie. She seems content as ever, in this situation, and I realise I don't know what her original plans were, or if she had any. I should have asked.

She and Mum disappear together out of the front door. I guess they can only be going to the Mowhay, or the cottage, neither of which would be ideal for giving birth! I think of the carefully written plan I've made, which is of course at home, alongside my half-packed hospital bag. I groan.

"Are you OK, Alice?" Karen asks, concerned.

"Yes, sorry, that was a groan of frustration. How bloody annoying this is!"

"I just hope Sam gets here in time."

"Me too, me too."

When Mum and Lizzie return, they are both smiling.

"I see you two are in cahoots with each other now," I say.

"Well, you were right, Alice, with your dressing-down!" I blush. I hadn't really meant to get on my high horse. "Anyway, Lizzie had already somehow had the foresight to make provision for this eventuality."

"Have you swallowed a dictionary, Sue?" Julie asks cheekily, and it makes me laugh.

"That's enough from you, young lady. What I'm trying to say is, Lizzie's already got the front room in the cottage set up for you, Alice. In fact, it's beautiful! You should come and see for yourself."

I am helped to my feet by Julie and Karen, although I don't really need any help, but it makes them feel better to be doing something practical, I think.

"What are you lot up to?" Dad asks. Ben is sitting on his knee now, trying on his glasses.

"Oh, just popping over to the cottage," I say. "You stay here with Grandpa, OK, Ben?"

"OK, Mummy." I don't think he had any intention of coming over, anyway.

Lizzie opens the cottage door for me, and I go in first, followed by Julie, Karen, Mum, and finally Lizzie herself.

The lounge has been transformed. There is a fire just taking hold in the hearth, and the floor and settee have been covered with towels, old sheets, and duvet covers, from our charity bags. Sophie's old Winnie the Pooh bean bag is by the fire, surrounded by cushions. The warm air is gently scented with lavender, and something else I can't place, but which Lizzie says is clary sage ("Together, they can help promote relaxation, and contractions," she says. "And don't worry, they're perfectly safe for you and your baby.")

The candles which we'd taken to the Mowhay are placed on the windowsills and doorways, and, together with the light from the fire, they breathe a soft warmth into the room.

"I was tempted to get out the old paddling pool, as a birthing pool, but I thought better of it," Lizzie laughs.

"Very wise," I say, "I don't much fancy giving birth in green mouldy water!"

"But I can run the bath, if you want one at any point," she says.

"Or I can," Mum interjects. I give her a look. "Or any of us," she quickly adds.

"And don't worry, I've used the actual bags from all this stuff to protect the flooring, and the furniture," Lizzie says. "So it's a bit of a mess upstairs, to be honest, but don't think about all that now. I'll pack it all up again and take it to the shop when it's open."

"Lizzie!" I say. "You don't need to worry about that. I am just… so… grateful…" I can feel the beginnings of another contraction. "Honestly." I hug her. "You are a marvel."

"Yes, Lizzie, you are," says Mum, which makes me smile.

I sit out the pain and then we trudge back across to the house. I am not ready for my personal birthing suite yet. The air outside is warmer now, even though the dark of night is already creeping close. I just hope Sam is here soon. When I get in, I phone him, and Sophie answers. "We've just stopped to get some fuel. We're on the A30. I think we'll be another hour or so, Dad says."

An hour sounds doable. Back in the house, we all sit together to watch the latest Julia Donaldson adaptation, which is followed by one of the Shrek films. It's a good excuse for some downtime for us all, but I am finding it hard to sit still, and it does not escape me that one or other of my parents regularly casts a concerned glance my way.

"I might head over to the cottage," I say. "Just to chill out a bit. Do you mind?"

"Do you want me to come with you?" Mum says.

"No, that's fine. Honestly, if you can stay here with Ben and keep him entertained, that will be brilliant. I feel like I'm missing huge chunks of his Christmas, though."

"He's having a whale of a time! And this is what it's all about, isn't it? Extended family. Getting together. Ben might be too young to remember this Christmas, but I bet that if he does, it will be happy memories."

"I hope so."

"Now you go on, get a bit of peace and quiet. I'll have my phone on, so just call or text if you need me."

22

Under a clear sky, I walk cautiously towards my old home, grateful for some time to myself. I open the door to the cottage, and I breathe in the aroma of wood smoke, lavender and clary sage. In the peace and solitude of the lounge I sit, bringing my legs up onto the settee, and leaning back against the stack of pillows. Astoundingly, I fall asleep, though not fully, and I'm aware of the occasional noise of a log shifting in the fire. Knowing that Ben is being so well looked after, by some of the people I love most in the world, means I can give myself permission to relax, and think about me. How did Lizzie know this might happen? I wonder. Is she some kind of witch?

I'm convinced she really might be, as she enters the house just as I'm thinking this. "Yes, she's here. I'll hand you over," she is saying into the work phone.

"Alice?" It's not Sam, as I'd hoped, but Sandi. "How are you doing, love?"

"I'm alright. I just had a little snooze, in fact, but—" I have to break off as pain grips me – "yes, I think that's the worst one yet. Are you coming up here?"

"I'm going to try, my love. Your father-in-law's just been telling me about his friend with the snow plough. He's trying to get hold of him, to get me a lift!"

Poor old Bill. Some Christmas for him! Still, I'd be very grateful if he could get her to me.

"I'm on the phone for now, though, whenever you need me, or get your Mum, or your friend, to call me, OK?"

"OK. Thank you."

"Shall I go again?" asks Lizzie.

"No, that's fine. It might be nice to have some company now."

"Should I get your mum?" she half-turns to go.

"No. You'll do nicely, thank you. And I'm sure Mum will make her own way across sometime soon!" I laugh. "But how did you know, Lizzie, to do all this?"

"You'll never believe me," she says.

The wind, which I had not noticed on my way across, blows down the chimney, making the flames flicker.

"Alright," Lizzie says, but I have the feeling she is not talking to me. "Alright," she says soothingly. I could swear that the fire is calm again. "Would you believe me," she says tentatively, "if I told you it was Elizabeth?"

I am thrown for a moment. She wants to be called Elizabeth? She's always been Lizzie. I'm sure that's how she introduced herself.

"From the beach," she says, to clarify. "Elizabeth Grayley."

"It was...?" I am lost for words.

"Yes. I know... I understand you may not believe this. It's very hard to take in, if you're not sure about these things. But I went to see her, yesterday, like I told you I was going to do. She's been trying to get your attention, you know. That owl. I thought it was odd. And the lights...?"

"The Christmas tree?"

"Yes."

I'm not sure about this, at all. But how could Lizzie have known about the Christmas tree lights?

"She says she tried to connect with you, when you were alone. But she was worried she'd scared you."

I think back rapidly. Was anyone else there any of the

times that it had happened? Only Meg, I think.

"The dog!" Lizzie laughs. "Yes, she knows she spooked Meg, and she's sorry. She didn't mean to."

A chill runs through me now. I can't tell if it's fear, or thrill.

"Is she… is she here now?"

The flames flicker again.

"Does that answer your question?"

I try to stand up. "This is…?"

"I'm sorry, Alice. Maybe it's too much. My god, your mum'll kill me."

"No, no, she won't," I say, beginning to pace. "Because I'm not going to tell her."

"Do you believe me, Alice?" Lizzie is looking at me questioningly.

"I don't know," I say. "I don't know. I know you believe it. But…" I'm struck dumb by another pain. "I don't know."

"It's fine, it's fine," Lizzie is at my side, rubbing my back. "And it really doesn't matter either way. Look, I'm going to get your mum."

"No, don't leave me alone here!" I exclaim, scared that what Lizzie said might be true, and having no idea what I think about that. "Just phone her. She'll be straight over."

It doesn't seem to take long for the contractions to really gain speed, and increase in frequency, though I think I lose all sense of time, really. I kind of go into myself, so that I can find a way to cope with the intense pain that takes hold of me with each 'tightening', as Sandi is calling them.

"She's on her way," Mum says. "Sandi, I mean. With Bill."

"Good old Bill," I smile, and then start laughing, almost deliriously. "Old Bill," I explain.

Mum smiles, though I think she's humouring me. "You're doing so well, Alice, my love. So well. Just hold on. Keep going."

"Well, which one is it?" I say, through gritted teeth. "Hold on, or keep going?" I am actually attempting another joke here, but Mum just looks upset. "Sorry, Mum. I'm just… trying… to get through it."

The four women seem to be in and out of the room, doing what, I don't quite know. In turns holding my hand, or offering me water, rubbing my back, trying to find me a comfortable position. Was it this painful with Ben? I don't remember.

"I… want it… out!" I wail.

Then I'm aware of a different voice. A strong, sure voice, who brings me back out into the room. "Don't you worry, it's coming out!" she says.

"Sandi!" I could cry at the sight of her. As well-meaning as everyone else is, none of them have the experience or confidence to do what needs to be done. And to take charge of me so I have somebody's lead to follow. Until now, it's like I've been trying to feel my way in the dark.

Sandi expertly takes a look, with the minimum of fuss. "Oh, you're not too far off, Alice. Not far at all. And your mum tells me you're doing so well. They're all very proud of you, these four. And you should be proud of them, too. They've stuck with you, you know."

I look at the four shining faces, behind Sandi. It is dark behind them, and it makes me think of the Queen *Bohemian Rhapsody* video, which makes me want to laugh again. "We will not let you go," I murmur.

"That's right," Mum says. "We wouldn't let you go, Alice." I haven't the heart to tell her I was reciting song lyrics. She looks close to tears, if truth be told, and I try to harness my sense of the present, and reality. I do not wish to upset my mum, and it must be so hard for her, seeing her only child in pain, even though she knows why, and that it is all for a good reason in the long run.

"Why don't you four go and have something to eat?" I suggest. "Now Sandi's here. You all deserve a rest."

"*You* deserve a rest, Alice," Julie says. For a moment, I wonder how this is for her, knowing how much she has wished to be pregnant, yet it hasn't happened for her. Zinnia came from an entirely different place, but the adoption is no less wonderful than giving birth.

"I'll get one!" I laugh. I can feel another contraction is on its way. "Go on," I say. "You won't miss anything. We won't let you, will we, Sandi?"

"But Sandi can't leave you, Alice."

"No, but we can phone, and you can come straight over…" It's too much, and I can talk no longer. Then Sandi, who has been unpacking her bag, is handing me a mask, and instructing me to put it over my mouth and nose, and breathe, and suddenly I don't feel nearly as much pain as I did. And I'm light-headed, and dreamy. It feels good.

I am dimly aware of the room emptying, so that it is now just me, and Sandi, and I have my *drishti*, as Lizzie calls it in yoga. A point of focus.

"You hold onto that mask if you can, Alice, and breathe, OK? When you feel another one coming on, put it over your mouth and your nose, and just breathe."

The room feels calmer now, and I don't know if it's the gas and air, Sandi's presence, the absence of the others, or all three of these things. The tightness subsides, and Sandi takes the chance to check my blood pressure.

"You're doing lovely, Alice. Nothing to worry about here."

I am so relieved.

"Now you need to tell me, now the others aren't here, who you want in here with you when things really get going."

"You mean they haven't really got going yet?" I ask, dismayed. How much more pain can my body provide? How much more can I take?

"Oh now, they're well on their way, believe me. But in the moment – you know, *that* moment – who do you want by your side?"

"Sam!" I say.

"I know, I know, and I hope he gets here in time. But just in case he doesn't–" I know when I'm being placated – "who do you want to be here?"

"My mum," I say. "Mum."

"That's fine. That's what I thought you'd say. And I can say, as a mother of grown-up daughters myself, what an absolute honour she'll consider it. That is if Sam doesn't get here in time, of course."

"Of course."

It feels like no time at all until the next one. Heat goes through me, right up my neck and across my face. I close my eyes. Grit my teeth.

"That's it. That's a girl," Sandi says. She presses the mask into my hand. "Breathe through it."

I am so grateful to Lizzie for the beautiful surroundings she's created. Every now and then, I am myself enough to appreciate them. But I am missing Sam, so much, and desperate for him to be here. Can I hold on? Can I use my inner strength and determination to keep our baby inside until he gets here?

"Can you call Sam please, Sandi?" I ask.

"Of course, my love. Of course. I might have to take the phone outside, though, my signal's rubbish in here."

I don't care, I just need to know where he is.

"Remember, if you have another contraction, gas and air."

"Gas and air," I repeat.

"There's a girl."

I hear the click of the front door, and I'm alone. I try to push myself up, to get a bit more comfortable, but I cry out with pain, and I drop the bloody mask, and before I know it, another contraction is upon me.

"Sandi!" I say, but I can just make out her voice outside. She must be talking to Sam, at least, I think, but then I'm deep inside it, and I'm holding on for all I'm worth, while my body tenses, and I want to buck and cast the pain aside. Then Sandi's with me and she's holding my hand, and I'm squeezing hers, and so glad to have this physical comfort, and that I'm not alone anymore. And again it starts to ease, and I open my eyes, feeling the grip on my hand loosen, but there is nobody else in the room with me. And the flames flicker in the fire, and I don't know what else to think except that Elizabeth was here.

Sandi is with me in moments. "Oh, my love," she says, collecting the mask from the floor and putting it into my hands. "Don't tell me you had another one?"

"I did."

"Well, the good news is, Sam thinks he'll be here soon. And I'm not just saying that," she says. "I'm afraid he's had to beg a lift from Bill as well. We'd better get that man a nice bottle of whisky to say thank you for this. But your Sam's been trying to get the car up here, but the roads are too icy. It's got cold out there again, you know. Frozen the melted snow good and proper."

"Is it a clear night?"

"It is now, yes. It's lovely."

"Could you open the curtains, do you think, please?"

"Of course I can, if that's what you want."

I lean against the pillows, and look up and out of the small window. My view is narrow, but I can see a star or two, and I ask Sandi to turn off some of the candles so that I can make out the night sky more easily.

"Well, of course, but I'll just check how dilated you are first, shall I? It can't be long now."

This thought is bittersweet. That the pain won't last much longer is a huge relief. But that Sam might not get here in time is almost unbearable. I know the baby's got to come when it's ready, though.

"Oh my, Alice. You're really close now. I don't think I can turn those candles off. In fact, to be honest, I think I need a bit more light, really. Should I close the curtains, do you think?"

"Do whatever you need to do," I say, "and please can you ask Mum to come over?"

23

"Alice, my lovely girl," Mum says, stroking back my hair as she used to when I was little, and kissing my forehead. "You are doing so well, and we are so proud of you."

"Is Ben OK?"

"He is absolutely fine! Last time I checked, he was sound asleep in that big bed, and your dad had fallen asleep next to him!"

"He hadn't!" I manage a laugh.

"Yes, but I woke him up. We switched the light down low, and tiptoed downstairs. Zinnia's fast asleep, too. She's a lovely girl, isn't she?"

"She really is."

"Just like Julie."

"Yes," I say, "she really is."

Here we go again. Sandi gives Mum a nod, and my mum helps me to hold the mask to my face. I breathe, and I breathe, and I'm doing it too fast, and Sandi tells me to slow down. When it's over, Sandi says, "It's going to come soon, Alice. I'm afraid there'll be no stopping it when it's time, and I'm going to need you to do as I say, OK?"

"OK."

"So I'm going to keep you uncovered, from the waist down, from now on. And your mum's going to stay up that end with you, and I'll be down the business end."

I nod and laugh, and I'm scared and exhilarated, and even though I want Sam, now more than anything I want this baby in my arms.

On the next contraction, Sandi tells me to start pushing,

and I really do my best, but I'm so tired now.

"That was very good, Alice," she says. "I can see the top of a little head there. Which means that next time you've got to go for it again, OK?"

"OK." I grit my teeth.

Mum's face looks white, but her eyes are on mine, and the next time the pain comes I think I am ready for it, and I push for all I'm worth.

"That's it, that's it," says Sandi. "Keep going."

My mind is a whirl, and I try to keep focused. I think I see somebody move behind Mum. "Elizabeth," I say. I may be imagining her, I may be not, but either way it's fine. It makes me feel calm.

"No, Lizzie's at the other house. Do you want her?" Mum asks.

"No!" I start laughing. "No, Mum. Just you."

She looks pleased. And again it comes, and again. I don't know how many times. And I push, and Mum and Sandi encourage me, and then there is a cry, and I don't know if it is me, or Mum, or Sandi, or the baby. But it's out. The baby is out, and I'm crying, and Mum's crying, and Sandi is being efficient and organised, and checking the baby for vital signs, before she helps me pull aside my top and puts her – because it is a her – on my chest, and I've done it, and I'm holding my baby, with her skin on mine. All mottled and bloody and gunky and unbelievably beautiful.

"Alice?" The door is pushed tentatively open, and there he is, my beautiful golden Sam. He has missed his second daughter's birth by minutes, but it doesn't matter. My mum kisses me, and steps back. "I'll go and share the news," she says, tactfully.

Sam takes her place, and he looks at me, with tears running down his face. "I'm so sorry, Alice. So sorry I didn't make it in time. I let you down." But his eyes are already on her, our little girl, and I move so that he can see her better.

"You didn't, Sam, you made it just in time. She's here," I say, "and I've been so well looked after."

"Can I hold her?" he asks.

Sandi looks at me. "We'll need to get her into something a bit warmer," she says. I nod.

"Come on, Sam, let's find her some clothes."

"I don't have any," I say. "It's all back at the house."

"I brought it all," says Sam. "I went home to leave Sophie there while Bill was on his way, and I just threw it all in a bag. I didn't know what you'd need!"

Sandi helps him dress her, then she turns to me. "I'm afraid you're not quite done yet, Alice, I'm sorry."

Sam holds the baby, our baby, while Sandi helps me deliver the placenta. "That's it, Alice, and you have done so well. So very well. A Christmas baby! Do you know what you'll call her?"

"Holly?" Sam says, joking, but I look at him.

"I like it."

"Really?" he asks.

"Yes, really."

"Do you know what? I think I do, too. Holly Branvall," he says, trying it out for size.

"She sounds like a writer, or an actress," Sandi laughs.

There is a gentle knock at the door, and my mum is there with my dad. Karen and Ron are just behind. Sam doesn't even know his mum's got engaged, I think, but I'll leave it to Karen to share her good news. I've more than enough happiness of my own.

They come in and hug Sam, and look at Holly, and kiss me gingerly.

212

"Your dad wanted to wake Ben!" Mum says.

I must admit, it's crossed my mind, too. "Better not, I suppose, Dad. You know how grumpy he'll be. And you'll never get him back to sleep!"

"No, let Ben sleep," Karen says, "and let Alice concentrate on this little one. She's going to have to share her mummy from tomorrow."

I smile. She is right. Tonight, I am all Holly's.

The grandparents make way for friends, as Julie and Lizzie come in.

"Holly!" Julie says. "I love it."

"And you know I do," says Lizzie. "And a little bit of solace for the Holly King, now the Oak King's back in charge!"

Sam pulls a face behind her back, but he's only teasing. I don't know if he'll quite believe it if I tell him about all that's been happening, though. Or he'll find a rational explanation, of course. Now that I'm here, on the other side, so to speak, I don't quite know if I believe it, either, but I am sure I felt that hand in mine, when I needed it.

"How about Julie for a middle name?" my friend suggests.

"Elizabeth?" Lizzie asks, smiling at me.

"She's not naming her after you, Lizzie! I'm her best friend," Julie protests. "It can be Lizzie next time."

"Steady on!" I laugh. "I'm not sure there's going to be a next one. And anyway, I've already thought about this, and if Sam agrees, I have the perfect name, I think." I beckon him close, so I can whisper to him, and, even though he has no idea why I've chosen it, he loves it.

"Holly Rose Branvall," I say. "Welcome to the world."

24

Boxing Day morning is slow to start but once it does, it is light, bright and sunny, in sharp contrast to the previous days. The snow has all but gone, though the Secular Snow Singers cling bravely on. Meltwater drips from all directions and the birds are in full song, as though relieved by the turn that the weather has taken.

There are sore heads and happy smiles, and an almost shyness amongst us, like we've been through some huge adventure together. In a way, I suppose, we have.

Sam, Holly and I have spent a beautiful night in the glow of the fire and candles. While I lay shattered on the sofa, with my baby in my arms, Sam, Lizzie, Mum and Julie tidied the room around me. They whipped away the sheets and towels and plastic bags while I had a shower. Tending to the fire, and my every whim. I had cups of tea, hot buttered toast, a bowl of nuts and raisins, and some of the leftover fruit salad. They took it in turns to hold Holly while I ate, and I chewed, ravenously, replacing the energy I'd used.

Sandi had stayed for a while, keeping an eye on me and Holly. "My husband's got a 4x4, and he's borrowed some snow chains. He thinks he'll be able to make it up here now," she smiled. "I didn't want to ask Bill again. It sounds like he's done more than enough for today. And he'll be up feeding the cattle again at some ungodly hour."

"Please say sorry to your husband for ruining your Christmas!" I'd said.

"Oh, don't you worry about that. He's used to it. And anyway, you haven't ruined it. I love a Christmas baby!

214

Now you enjoy this evening, and any problems, you just call, OK? Otherwise, I'll be visiting you in a couple of days, and then it will be the health visitor."

"Thank you so much, Sandi."

"My pleasure." She had smiled, and was gone, and soon Julie and Mum were gone across to the house, and Lizzie upstairs. It was just me, Sam and Holly. We dozed, and woke, and ate, and I fed Holly, and we checked her nappy, and we just gazed and gazed at her. And we did a little bit of gazing at each other, too.

"I'm so sorry I let you down, Alice." Sam's eyes were on mine, searching.

"We've already been through this. You didn't let me down. I'm just sorry you missed the birth. Although… most of it is a blur now. I wish you'd been there for that. But the important thing is that you're here for her now, and every day after."

"I will be, I promise."

"I know."

The flames flickered, sending shapes dancing across the walls, and we had kissed, above our sweetly sleeping daughter's head, and then sunk back contentedly. Happy to take this one night of elated, unreal, magical bliss, before real life raised its head once more.

❄ ❄ ❄

In the morning, both Sam and I were desperate for Ben to meet his little sister. Sam kept checking on the house across the way, looking for signs of life. At ten to eight, he said, "They're up!" And he was out of the house before I'd even had a chance to reply.

Shortly afterwards, he returned, triumphant, with Ben

on his shoulders, stooping to get through the doorway and then swinging Ben down to the floor.

"Mummy!" Ben said, and ran to me, but stopped in his tracks at the sight of the strange little bundle in my arms.

"Hello, my lovely boy," I said, reaching an arm out for him so he could climb onto the settee and sit next to me. I pulled back the baby blanket so he could see his little sister properly. "Ben," I said, "meet Holly."

I realised, just a split second before his little face lit up and broke into a huge smile.

"Ben and Holly!" he shouted. Oh bugger. Why had I not thought of that? But I looked at her tiny face, and I knew it was the right choice for her. We will just have to deal with it.

Sam was laughing. "I got it last night," he said. "I just didn't want to ruin the moment."

"Smartarse!" I mouthed. He grinned. To Ben, I said, "Do you want to give Holly a kiss?"

He leaned ever-so-gently forwards, and kissed his sister on the nose. Her face twitched, but she didn't wake. I swelled with love and pride, and thoughts of a beautiful friendship blossoming between these two. I mean, there will be arguments, and plenty of them, I am sure, but now they have each other, and I hope they always will.

The others come over in dribs and drabs, Ron and Zinnia meeting Holly for the first time. Julie brings breakfast, Mum brings coffee.

"Decaf," she says proudly. "And I added a little sugar and cream, too."

"Oh my god, that tastes so good. Thank you, Mum."

Everything tastes extra good today.

After breakfast, I have a tentative bath, and then Sam,

Holly and I go across to the bigger house. "Your first outing!" I say to Holly, taking my time and hoping there's no surprise patches of ice anywhere. My body feels lighter, and it's strange trying to renegotiate my balance. When we push open the door to the holiday house, I think of coming downstairs yesterday morning, to find Lizzie's handiwork. It feels like that was weeks ago.

The place is already nearly back to how it had been on Christmas Eve, though the extra decorations which Lizzie put up have been left in place. There are bags packed in the hallway, and I can't believe how much stuff there is, given that this whole thing was entirely unplanned. Somehow, we seem to be leaving with an awful lot.

Dad and Julie walk to her car, to make sure it's definitely broken free from its freezing captor. They have a bit of work to do, but then she can drive to Amethi to pick up Dad, Ron and Sam and take them down to town so that they can collect their cars and bring them back up here. "After I've dropped you lot off, I'm taking Zinnie to Jim's, and we can finally see Luke! I'm so excited!"

"Saddo," I say, smiling. "Thank you, Julie, for everything. It's been a memorable Christmas."

"You can say that again."

"It's been a memorable Christmas."

"Very funny."

She kisses me, and then Holly. "You are beautiful," she whispers.

"Thanks, Julie."

"Not you, you ugly old crone. This little one. What do you think, Zinnie? Do you like her?"

"Yes," Zinnia says shyly, holding on to her mum's hand. "She's small."

"She certainly is," I say. "You go and have a lovely

Christmas with your daddy now, and your grandad, OK?"

"Alice, I can hear the office phone going!" Lizzie appears in the doorway, just after Julie's gone. "Shall I get it?"

Talk about being brought back to earth with a bump. I have put anything like work firmly out of my mind.

"Yes please, Lizzie, if you don't mind."

"Of course not."

She rushes off. She'll never make it in time, but hopefully they'll leave a message.

"How are you feeling, Alice?" Mum asks.

"I actually feel great!" I say. And it's true. I am tired, of course, but happily so.

"Your dad and I were wondering if you still wanted to come to us... stay tonight, let us look after you."

"Thank you, Mum," I say. "That is really lovely of you, but I think it might be better if we get home. He's shattered—" I say, nodding towards Ben, who is avidly watching *Paw Patrol*. Maybe being part of a real-life Ben and Holly has put him off his favourite programme – "and I am, too. And Sam. I'm really sorry, we'd love to be with you, too, but..."

"Say no more, Alice. You don't have to explain. You need to get back to your own place, and your own bed. I completely understand. It was only if you felt like being looked after for a little bit longer, that's all."

I hug her. "I love you, Mum."

"I love you, too. And your family. I can't believe it. My little girl."

"Mum!" I say, channelling my teenage self.

"Sorry! It just hits you sometimes. You'll find out yourself one day."

"It's true," Karen says. "Your children never stop being

your children. Even when they're fully grown adults, with kids of their own."

She is as happy as I've ever known her. She broke the news to Sam this morning, about her engagement, and he seemed genuinely delighted for her.

"I'll want you to give me away, Sam, you know. But Ron might want you for his best man..."

"Mum!" Sam had laughed. "I'm sure Ron's quite capable of finding his own best man. And I'll gladly give you away, if you promise you won't come back!"

She had looked at him askance for just a moment, but realised he was pulling her leg, and laughed. They've come a long way, these two.

When Lizzie returns, she has some notepaper with her. "There were two messages: one from the Barretts, who are on their way. And one from the Coopers, who say they're planning to come down today, too."

"Shit." I had not reckoned on this.

"Alice!" Mum says, moving her head meaningfully towards Ben.

"It's OK. He's not listening."

"Shall I call them back?" Lizzie asks.

"No, it's OK. Thank you, Lizzie. I'll do it. I just need to think..."

What am I going to do? I need to get home. I need to rest. And I really don't want to drag Julie back up here. Not today.

"I'll stay," Lizzie says. "If that's OK. I can let them in, and I can stay up here in the cottage, for a few days, in case they need anything. I'd let you know if there was a problem, so honestly, you can go home and stop thinking about work. This place is nearly as it was, and I can do any last

219

bits of cleaning. Just tell me what I need to know, and I'll do it."

"Are you sure?" I am thinking fast. Is there anything that Lizzie can't do? I don't think so. "There's one other lot of guests, who were meant to be coming. I need to phone and see what they're planning…"

"Just let me know where their details are, and I can phone them," says Lizzie.

"We'll need to change the sheets and covers, of course."

"I can do that," says Mum.

"We can do it together," says Karen.

"And clear the fireplace, and get more logs." Holly, secure in my arms, is blissfully unaware of the sudden change in activity level. Ben, eyes glued to the television, is happy to let it all go on behind him.

"I'll sort that," Lizzie says. "No problem."

"Erm…" What else?

"Alice," Karen lays a hand on my arm. "It's going to be fine. We can get this place back to just how it was. You go and phone them back. I'll hold Holly."

"OK. OK. Thank you, Karen."

"You know I'm dying to hold her anyway!"

I smile, and pass my tiny, sleeping baby safely into my mother-in-law's arms.

When I step outside, the sun is flooding Amethi with light, and glinting off the birdfeeder, which, recently vacated, is swinging to and fro. It feels strange already, not having Holly in my arms, but I know she is safe and sound, and surrounded by people who love her.

I climb the stairs to the office, and sigh as I sit in my desk chair. I am alone, and I realise it may be some time before I am again. Switching on the computer, I find the details of the Coopers and the Barretts, and I phone them, telling them they will be welcome at Amethi, but explaining that Lizzie will be there instead of me, and why.

"Oh my, a Christmas baby!" Mrs Cooper exclaims. "But are you sure that we can still come? I do feel like we've messed you around."

"It's hardly your fault!" I say. "I'm just sorry you've missed your Christmas dinner."

"Oh, we made do! And it was quite jolly, really. But we don't want to miss our trip to Cornwall entirely, if we can help it."

"I don't blame you!"

"We'll bring everything we need, so you get going, and enjoy this special time."

"I will."

The Barretts are only forty minutes away now, they tell me. They too offer congratulations when I tell them my news, and they tell me I don't need to worry about letting them in, or anything, in fact. They'll manage nicely, just the two of them. "We just want somewhere to tuck ourselves away for a few days. You won't hear a peep from us, I promise."

I end the call and I turn off my computer, too. I don't need to think any more about work now. I will be back to it soon enough. Then I sit for a just a few more minutes, letting everything settle around me. Contemplating the events of the past few weeks, and what the future might bring.

Be in the moment, I remind myself. But I need to just go back over the last twenty-four hours, it seems. I don't want to forget a thing, and I make myself try to recall the order of events. It all seems so surreal, and incredible, how everybody came together, and really carried me through.

I want to write it all down, but exhaustion is creeping up on me now. I can feel it, just behind my eyes, which are starting to feel sore. Breathing slowly, and deeply, I allow myself the luxury of just a few moments more, to help recharge my batteries, so that I am ready to rise to the challenges I'm sure are to come.

But I'm already starting to feel twitchy. I need to get back. The sound of a car approaching confirms this, and I stand and walk down the stairs, switching off the lights as I go.

"See you next year," I say to the empty space, then I walk out into the sunshine and back towards my family.

Acknowledgements

So… book eight! This was a surprise. Maybe less to you all than to me, as I know I've said more than once that I've finished this series and then ended up going back for more. I am genuinely working on *Maggie*, the second book of the Connections series, but I had a flash of inspiration that I'd like to write a Christmas book, and it seemed to fit very naturally with the Coming Back to Cornwall series, so here it is! Maggie had to step aside for a little while…

I don't know exactly how long it took to write but once I'd started, I tried to cram my writing into every spare moment, so this was the quickest I had ever written a book (in terms of weeks and days) and I was a little bit worried that it might actually just be rubbish. I am therefore extra grateful to my beta reading team, who answered my request, and met my fairly short timescale, and provided me with insightful, constructive and positive feedback. So thank you, in no particular order, to: Helen Smith, Marilynn Wrigley, Denise Armstrong, Rebecca Leech, Rosalyn Pengelly Osborn, Kate Jenkins, Sandra Francis, Amanda Tudor, Ginnie Ebbrell, Tracey Shaw, Alison Elizabeth, Yvonne Carpenter, Sheila Setter, Jean Crowe, Saxon Greenway and Lisa Coles. I know that there were technical issues for some of you, in terms of getting a copy of the book in time and I am very sorry about that. I would just like to thank all of you for your generosity in being willing to help me out in this way! I always get worried here that I have missed somebody out, so if I have, please, please feel free to shout at me, or send a strongly worded email in upper case letters.

Now, these books would not be what they are without

their beautiful covers. I owe a huge amount of thanks to my great friend Catherine Clarke, for always coming up with the goods, and for knowing what will look amazing. This time around, she sent me the draft and I asked her to do some other colour combinations, then ended up sticking with the first one she'd sent. Which just goes to show, she knows exactly what she's doing (but don't tell her that, I don't want her to get a big head).

I also have to thank my brilliant proofreader, Hilary Kerr, who I still have yet to meet in person (hopefully one day) and who, as well as offering great editorial tips as well as correcting my errors, has been able to offer canine advice too, which is an amazing bonus!

And I have another proofreader, in the shape of my dad, Ted Rogers, whose pernickety pedantry is really finding its niche! Thank you, Dad, for all your help and support.

As always, I'd also like to thank all my family and my friends, for keeping life fun and interesting, despite the time we are living through. 2020... 2021... two years I think many of us would rather forget. But I hope we've had good things from them, too. And I look forward to 2022 with a little trepidation. Let's see what it might bring. I can't say I am optimistic, or pessimistic. Maybe just curious, and hopeful!

To all of you readers, I am so very grateful to you all, for taking the time to read my books and to those of you who comment on my posts and ads on Facebook, or email me. It is hard to say how much of an honour it is to think of people enjoying my books. Whatever I say sounds disingenuous, but honestly, I feel very privileged.

I wish you all a happy Christmas, as happy as it can be, and I hope for us all that 2022 might just be a better year. Kath x

The full Coming Back to Cornwall series:

Book One of the Connections series
(Book Two coming soon):

What dark secrets could a harmless old lady possibly know?

Elise Morgan is nearly ninety years old. She loves her family, the sea, and night-time walks. She hates gossip, and bullies, and being called 'sweet', or treated like she's stupid, or boring (and sometimes like she's deaf), just because she has lived a long time.

Elise was sent to an all-girls' school, which was evacuated to Cornwall in the Second World War. She never left the county. She is an orphan, a mother, a grandmother, and a widow. Since her children moved away and her best friend died, life has seemed increasingly empty.

These days, she spends a lot of time sitting at her window, looking out at the world, as if nothing ever happens, and nothing ever has. To passers-by, she might seem just an old lady, but of course there is no such thing.

There was once a time when she lived a lot... and there are things she has never forgotten...

Elise **is the first book in the Connections series: a group of stories whose protagonists' lives are inescapably interwoven, in the Cornish town they call home.**

Writing the Town Read - Katharine's first novel.

"I seriously couldn't put it down and would recommend it to anyone to doesn't like chick lit, but wants a great story."

Looking Past - a story of motherhood, and growing up without a mother.

"Despite the tough topic the book is full of love, friendships and humour. Katharine Smith cleverly balances emotional storylines with strong characters and witty dialogue, making this a surprisingly happy book to read."

Amongst Friends - a back-to-front tale of friendship and family, set in Bristol.

"An interesting, well written book, set in Bristol which is lovingly described, and with excellent characterisation. Very enjoyable."

Coming Back to Cornwall in audio

The whole Coming Back to Cornwall series is being made into audiobooks so you can now listen to the adventures of Alice, Julie and Sam while you drive, cook, clean, go to sleep… whatever, wherever!

Printed in Great Britain
by Amazon

69605034R00139